others in the An...
by l...

# Death Rides an Ill Wind

"WBZE morning DJ and station manager Kelly Ryan is back, and the Caribbean Island sleuth's return couldn't come soon enough for me. Kelly is an outstanding heroine . . . independent and intelligent, yet her vulnerabilities peek through. . . . The strength of the Kelly Ryan mysteries is . . . [in] the island lifestyle and the interactions of Kelly's group of friends . . . I'd love to pull up a chair under the faded yellow canvas umbrella at their permanently reserved table overlooking the St. Chris harbor. . . . Riveting descriptions."  —*The Mystery Reader*

"A lively tale told with cynical good humor . . . Kelly and company are interesting and amusing, and their antics keep the pages turning."  —*Romantic Times*

"A good read."  —*BookBrowser*

# Death Dances to a Reggae Beat"

"I loved author Kate Grilley's debut, *Death Dances to a Reggae Beat*. . . . If you like a mystery where complex characterizations take center stage . . . and an unusual setting comes alive before your very eyes, then I definitely recommend *Death Dances to a Reggae Beat*".

—*The Mystery Reader*

*Kelly Ryan mysteries by Kate Grilley*

**DEATH DANCES TO A REGGAE BEAT**
**DEATH RIDES AN ILL WIND**
**DEATH LURKS IN THE BUSH**

# Death Lurks in the Bush

## Kate Grilley

BERKLEY PRIME CRIME, NEW YORK

This is a work of fiction. Names, characters, places, and incidents either are the product of the author's imagination or are used fictitiously, and any resemblance to actual persons, living or dead, business establishments, events, or locales is entirely coincidental.

### DEATH LURKS IN THE BUSH

A Berkley Prime Crime Book / published by arrangement with the author

PRINTING HISTORY
Berkley Prime Crime mass-market edition / July 2002

Visit our website at
www.penguinputnam.com

ISBN: 0-425-18549-4

Berkley Prime Crime Books are published
by The Berkley Publishing Group,
a division of Penguin Putnam Inc.,
375 Hudson Street, New York, New York 10014.
The name BERKLEY PRIME CRIME and the BERKLEY PRIME CRIME
design are trademarks belonging to Penguin Putnam Inc.

PRINTED IN THE UNITED STATES OF AMERICA

10  9  8  7  6  5  4  3  2  1

*For Dick and Julia Hyll*
*. . . here's to twenty-five years of*
*"Good friends and good times in the Caribbean"*
*(you know the rest)*

# Chapter
# 1

THE NEWS THAT a Very Important Person was coming to St. Chris was the biggest thing to hit our little Caribbean island since Hurricane Gilda.

Four months after Gilda, electrical power, phones, and cable TV were finally restored island-wide. We had power and phones in Isabeya and at WBZE in mid-November; but it wasn't until December thirty-first—Old Year's Day on the St. Chris calendar—that my house on the east end, one of the very last to receive electrical current, was back on line.

When I pulled into my driveway after a long, liquid lunch at the Watering Hole, I was greeted by an Oklahoma lineman. "Ma'am," he said in a honey-warm accent that would have melted icebergs in Alaska, "if you'd mosey inside and flip your breaker, I think we've got you connected." The lineman departed with a bottle of lukewarm Heineken from the stash in the chillbox I called my freezer, and warm wishes for a Happy New Year ringing in his ears.

I didn't know what to do first. What I really wanted most of all was a long, hot shower. At midnight I rang in the New Year in a blaze of light that made the Times Square ball drop look like a flickering candle.

Except for a smattering of blue FEMA tarp roofs on the slowly greening hillsides, and the dawn-to-dusk din of construction, life on St. Chris was almost back to normal. But the trees and plants, knocked silly by Gilda, were still storm stressed and didn't know whether to bloom or go dormant. The poinsettias in our gardens stayed stubbornly green through Christmas, while the African tulip trees that usually blossomed in May were decked with orange flowers in mid-December.

The airport runways and cruise ship dock had been repaired in record time. Our little island was thronged with high-season tourists escaping the icy blasts of winter to sun on St. Chris's beaches, frolic in tepid ocean, and bargain-hunt in Isabeya's duty-free shops.

The first inkling of the Big News came from Margo on a Friday morning in late January. "Kel, you'd better show up in town for lunch today. Jerry just called from Government House and he's got dirt."

"I'm all ears. Tell me now."

"He wouldn't tell me. The cad. Says he wants to see our faces when we hear it. I'll meet you at the round table. Get to town as fast as you can when your shift is over."

"It's payday at WBZE. When I'm off the air at noon I've got to sign checks for the troops, then stop at the bank. I should be at the Watering Hole by twelve-thirty."

"Be there or be square." Margo hung up on me, still laughing at her own wit.

I slid into my captain's chair at the Watering Hole round table at twelve forty-five.

"You're late, Kel," said Margo, tapping her watch with a manicured nail.

"Long bank line, sweetie." I scanned the immediate area. "Where's our resident gossipmonger?"

"He'd better get his butt here pretty quick," said Abby, checking her own watch. "I'm due in court at one-thirty. Margo and I have already ordered. I'm starving."

"Abby, you're always hungry. How many miles did you run this morning?"

"Only three, but I was running late."

Margo and I groaned. Abby grinned.

"What are you two having for lunch?" I asked.

"Chef's salad with extra bleu cheese dressing."

"I had that yesterday. What's the special?"

"Turn around, Kel, the specials are on the chalkboard behind you," said Margo, adding under her breath, "where they always are."

Carole, the Watering Hole waitress, arrived at the table with lunch for Margo and Abby, then turned to take my order.

"I'll have an iced tea, and the Reuben special, and a white-on-white on the rocks for Jerry."

"You want Jerry's drink on your tab?"

"Sure. Why not, it's payday."

"Better your tab than his. His tops first prize in the St. Chris lottery."

"Hold up on Jerry's drink until I give you the signal."

Carole nodded and went back to the bar.

The bell in the Anglican church was tolling one when we spotted Jerry bustling along the cobblestone walk leading from Kongens Gade, Isabeya's main street, to the Watering Hole.

"Jerry, if your chest was puffed out any further, pigeons would be roosting on it," said Abby.

"I ordered a drink for you," I said, "but you don't get it until you tell us the news."

"Dish, Jerry," said Margo, poking his arm with her salad fork.

Jerry looked around the table, with a cat-that-ate-the-canary grin on his face. "You can't breathe a word of this to anyone until it's official."

We held our breath and waited.

Jerry motioned to us to move closer to him. "Guess who's coming here next month?"

No one said a word.

"The Queen." Jerry sat back in his chair, smugly awaiting our reactions.

"Very funny, Jerry," said Abby, shifting her focus back to her salad bowl.

"What Queen?" I asked before attacking my sandwich.

"Out with it, Jerry," Margo said, brandishing her fork.

"The Queen of Denmark is coming to St. Chris."

On an island where a visit from Ronald McDonald was an event that drew a standing-room-only crowd, Jerry's announcement was Really Big News.

Margo dropped her fork. Her hands went to the top of her head as if she were adjusting a tiara, and a beatific smile lit her face. "This will be so good for the island." Visions of real estate sales danced in her head.

"How do you know this?" I asked Jerry.

"I overheard Chris, the governor's aide, on the phone this morning," he replied. "Where's my drink?"

"When is she coming? For how long? Details, Jer, I want details."

"A month from tomorrow. She'll be here for Ag Fair weekend."

"Start practicing your curtsies, ladies." Abby put down her napkin and reached for her briefcase. "I've got to go, I'm late for court."

I motioned to Carole to bring Jerry his drink, then excused myself from the table. "Back in a sec, guys, I need to make a pit stop." I couldn't wait to get to a phone to call Miss Maude.

She answered on the first ring.

"Kelly, I am so glad you phoned. Can you keep a secret? I had the most exiting news from Copenhagen this morning. Queen Margrethe is coming to St. Chris! I really must go. I have something on the stove that needs attending. Come by tomorrow morning for a swizzle at eleven."

I hung up to find Margo standing next to me.

"Who were you calling?"

"Miss Maude, but don't tell Jerry."

"I won't tell if you won't. Have you got another quarter? I want to call Paul."

By midafternoon all of St. Chris was buzzing with the news of the Royal Visit.

# Chapter 2

IN 1917, WHEN the red and white Dannebrog was lowered for the last time, St. Chris ceased to be a Danish colony after two hundred years under Danish rule.

Ties with Denmark were not easily severed. Danish West Indian currency remained in circulation on St. Chris until 1934. Under the terms of the 1917 transfer, all St. Chris residents were given one year to decide whether they wished to retain their Danish citizenship. It was a simple process, requiring only a declaration before the court that one wished to remain a Dane. Parents were allowed to decide for children under eighteen.

Miss Maude, our beloved retired schoolteacher and one of the last declared Danes still living on St. Chris, was a young girl on Transfer Day and often told the story of wearing a new pink dress the day the Dannebrog was lowered from the flagstaff on the green near Fort Frederick in Isabeya, seeing tears in her parents' eyes, and the jumping-up-and-down excitement of the children when ice cream was served in the gazebo bandstand after the ceremonies. She described the day so vividly I could close my eyes and feel I'd actually been there.

After Transfer Day her family moved from Isabeya into the native stone house near the west end rain forest where Miss Maude grew up, was married in the garden, raised a daughter, and has lived ever since.

I pulled into her driveway a few minutes before eleven to find the Saturday morning rum swizzle party already in progress. Sitting in cushioned wicker chairs on the front gallery were Miss Lucinda, Benjamin and his wife Camille, and Miss Maude's granddaughter Amelia. Miss Maude rocked slowly in her favorite teak rocker, the same chair in which she'd been nursed as an infant. I heard voices in the adjoining fruit tree orchard, and turned to see Trevor, Benjamin and Camille's eight-year-old son, playing hide-and-seek with Amelia's kids. I waved to the children as I headed up the short flight of steps to the gallery.

I hugged Miss Maude, then took a seat next to Camille on the wicker settee.

On a low table in front of us were a glass pitcher of swizzles already depleted to the halfway mark, a full ice bucket, an empty glass, and a plate of cheese straws. I helped myself to a drink, first filling my glass with lots of ice to water down the rum—ice cubes had been worth their weight in diamonds after Gilda and we were still getting used to the luxury of having as many cubes as we wanted—then edged my fingers toward the cheese straws before Miss Lucinda emptied the plate.

A copy of the *Coconut Telegraph*, the St. Chris daily newspaper, lay on the table. THE QUEEN IS COMING!, trumpeted the Saturday morning front-page headline. The Big News, no longer a Big Secret, was the only topic of conversation.

"Now that we're all here," said Miss Maude, smiling

at her family and friends, "I have a small announcement to make. I shall be entertaining Queen Margrethe and Prince Henrik at a small dinner party during the royal visit and you are all invited."

I don't know about anyone else, but my heart began thumping. Me? Having dinner with the Queen? Wow.

In the hubbub following Miss Maude's invitation, one voice stood out.

"I think that's very sensible of you, Maude," said Miss Lucinda. "It'll be the only decent meal they'll have on St. Chris. Everyone knows the food at Government House is abominable. No wonder the governor drinks so much. He's an embarrassment to us all and should be hung out to dry." Miss Lucinda concluded her pronouncement with an emphatic nod, then reached for the swizzle pitcher.

I felt the wicker settee begin to wobble and knew Camille was close to losing it. I focused on my own glass, not daring to risk eye contact or I'd burst out laughing.

Miss Maude was no slouch in dealing with the unruly. Using the same diversionary tactics she'd honed in the classroom, she turned to us and said with a twinkle in her eye, "The children must be thirsty. Camille, there's a pitcher of limeade in the refrigerator. Kelly, you'll find a stack of paper cups on the kitchen counter." It was the social equivalent of being banished to the cloakroom or sent to the principal's office.

Once Camille and I were safely in the kitchen, the laughter we'd tried to suppress erupted. We clung to each other for support.

"Out of the mouths of babes," I said as we both wiped tears from our faces. "Miss Lucinda really tells it like it is. I wish I had her nerve." Our present governor is a widower with a rumored fondness for the leading St. Chris export. Preferably the 151 proof variety. I couldn't remember the last time I'd seen the governor in public. But then I didn't travel in Government House circles.

"Have you heard the news about Miss Maude?" Camille whispered.

"What news?" I whispered back.

"She's being given a special honor by the Queen."

"Wow."

"I think that's the real reason for the dinner party."

"How wonderful for Miss Maude," I said. "She must be thrilled. How did you find out?"

"Ben's in charge of local security for the royal visit." Camille glanced over her shoulder. "*Sh-h-h.* I hear someone coming."

Camille grabbed the cups and pitcher of limeade and headed out the kitchen door for the side yard.

Benjamin entered the kitchen. "Miss Maude sent me for another glass. Chris Edwards just arrived from Government House. Kelly, before we leave I want to talk to you about the homestead house. The building committee needs your help."

"You don't want me, Benjamin. Remember what happened with last year's Navidad de Isabeya parade committee? I'm as welcome on a committee as the thirteenth fairy at a christening. Ask someone else."

"Lightning never strikes in the same place twice."

"You wanna bet on that?"

Benjamin took a clean glass from the cupboard and headed back toward the gallery. "I'm not letting you off the hook, Kelly. Come to the fairground tomorrow at eleven and bring a hammer. Bring Michael, too. We need some muscle on this project."

When we returned to the front gallery, Chris had appropriated Benjamin's chair next to Miss Maude's rocker.

"Hey, Chris," I said, resuming my place on the settee, "What brings you out on a Saturday morning?" It was pretty obvious from his attire, straight out of the Greg

Norman collection including the shark logo embroidered in multicolored thread on his wide-brimmed black straw hat, that Chris was headed for the golf course. A chamois-shined black Government House car was parked alongside the road. The tinted windows made it too dark to see inside the car. I wondered if Chris had driven himself or used one of the staff drivers.

"I came to talk with Maude," he replied, flashing a disarmingly boyish smile. Turning to his hostess, he added, "I should have phoned first but I was on my way to the club, big golf tournament this weekend, and thought I'd stop by. I didn't realize you were having company."

"Not company, Christopher. Family and friends. You are always welcome to join us," said Miss Maude. "Please help yourself to a drink and some cheese straws."

A yellow-green lizard scampered across the table to flick the last crumb from the plate of cheese straws. Clinging to the edge of the plate with tiny toes that looked as delicate as the veins in a newly sprouted leaf, he cocked his head and looked at us through shiny black eyes.

Miss Maude turned to her oldest friend. "Lucy dear, would you mind fetching the tin from the kitchen? The refreshment plate needs refilling."

Miss Lucinda looked down at her feet, clad in cerise leather shoes adorned with straps crossing the puffy flesh of her insteps. One could almost picture her as a young girl wearing black patent leather Mary Janes. "Maude, you know I would. But these shoes are new and they're still a bit snug." She topped off her glass and sat back in her chair, gazing at Chris with the intensity of a nearsighted owl. I heard her mumble "You look like my David," before taking a healthy swig of her freshened drink.

Amelia quickly picked up the plate. "I'll do it, Granny Maude."

Chris took a sip of his drink, then said, "I want to talk

to you about the schedule for the royal visit."

When he uttered the last two words, he had everyone's undivided attention. We all leaned forward in our chairs. Amelia came back from the kitchen with the replenished plate, which she placed on the table just out of Miss Lucinda's reach.

Chris continued. "We expect the royal party to arrive early Saturday morning four weeks from today. There will be a brief welcoming ceremony at the Isabeya dock, followed by a walking tour of Isabeya, then the ribbon-cutting ceremony at the fair and the dedication of the homestead house. Our distinguished guests will be escorted to lunch at Government House followed by an afternoon reception in the Government House garden, where you will be presented to the Queen and the award ceremony will take place. That evening there will be a formal dinner at Government House to honor you and our royal guests. I think that pretty much covers it." He smiled at the group, then polished off his drink and set the empty glass on the table.

Miss Maude gestured to the plate of cheese straws. "I know our visitors will enjoy the day that has been planned for them. However, it's already been arranged that the dinner that evening will be here, not at Government House."

Chris was caught with a mouthful of food. We all waited until he swallowed and wiped the crumbs from his mouth. "I didn't see that on the agenda."

Miss Maude said quietly but firmly, "I have known the Queen since she was an infant. I attended her wedding to Prince Henrik and was last entertained by them when I was in Denmark in August before the hurricane. It was then that we first discussed the royal visit and I extended to them my invitation to dinner. They were quite pleased about it. I had a letter from the Queen at Christmas confirming the arrangements."

"Obviously I had no idea other plans had been made. But what about security?"

Benjamin spoke up. "I'll see to it, Chris. I'm in charge of security for the entire visit."

"Your guests will, of course, have to go through a security clearance," said Chris.

"It will be an evening of family and the dear friends who have become my extended family." Miss Maude smiled at the little group seated on the gallery. "My dining table seats twelve. I would be honored if you and the governor would join us that evening."

"That's very generous of you, Maude. I'll convey your invitation to the governor."

"The governor needs a wife," said Miss Lucinda. "If he remarried, maybe he wouldn't drink so much and he'd get out of Government House more often."

In the small silence that followed, Chris looked pointedly at his watch. "Can't be late for my tee time." He clasped Miss Maude's hand. "Thank you for your hospitality. We'll talk again. Soon."

# Chapter
# 3

"LEAVE IT TO you, Kel, to have a dinner party where everyone else does the cooking." Margo inspected a batter-dipped shrimp before plunging it into a fondue pot filled with bubbling oil.

"Busy hands are happy hands," I replied, reaching for a ceramic flask of hot saki. "Saki, anyone?"

"Sock it to yourself," said Margo, spearing another shrimp. "Hands off the red-handled forks, guys, they're all mine." She leaned forward to peer into the pot. "How you know when this stuff is done?"

"When the batter puffs up and gets crispy," I said. "About two or three minutes."

Margo, Paul, Michael, and I were having Saturday night dinner on my refurbished gallery. The screened-in area I'd added to the house when I bought it had gone bush during Gilda, leaving behind only a bare concrete slab. After living with the slab for a couple of months while I waited for the insurance check, I decided that when I rebuilt, I'd expand the gallery to include space for a dining table and chairs and also make it as hurricane-proof as possible. The result was an area bigger than my inside living room, topped with a concrete roof, with wrought iron grillwork on three sides—much easier to maintain than cat-clawed screens—and included built-in hurricane shutters I could close with one hand.

"Mama, I can't handle that saki stuff. It tastes like warm turpentine." Michael headed for the kitchen, calling over his shoulder. "Who wants a cold beer?"

"Bring one for me," said Paul.

"I'll have white wine," said Margo.

"Good," I said, placing the saki flask next to my plate. "More for me." I stabbed a mushroom, coated it with tempura batter, and placed it in the pot to cook. "The green handles are mine."

Michael handed drinks around the table.

Margo sampled her wine. "This is good. I hope you have more of it." She glanced at my Charlie Brown Christmas tree standing in the corner of the gallery. "I love what you did with the gallery, but that tree is a disgrace. It's balder than Jerry. When are you going to take it down?"

"Sugar birds are nesting in it," I replied. "I may leave it up forever."

"It's a fire hazard. And it's ugly. Next year buy a plastic tree like everyone else. You buy it once, you have it forever."

"I like the smell of fresh pine."

Margo ignored me and continued her visual house tour. "You know, Kel, if you ever want to sell this place, you could make a fortune."

"Why would I want to sell? I spent years getting it whipped into shape. You remember what it was like when I bought it? You should. You sweet-talked me into it, you silver-tongued devil." I mimicked Margo's sales pitch.

" 'It's a fixer-upper, Kel, just needs a little TLC and a coat of paint.' Right, sweetie. It was a goat dung–infested ruin."

"If you ever change your mind, I want the listing."

It was time to nip Margo's sales pitch with one of my own. "After dinner we'll talk about the Island Palms Real Estate advertising contract on WBZE." I pointed to the fondue pot. "I think your shrimp is done."

Margo pulled her shrimp out of the pot and placed it on a paper plate to cool. "If the Queen shows up here for dinner, I hope you get out your best china instead of making her eat off paper plates."

"That's Miss Maude's problem," I said as I lifted my mushroom out of the oil, put it on my plate to cool, then speared a steak cube for my next morsel.

"Is the Queen having dinner at Miss Maude's?"

I nodded, my mouth too full of mushroom to speak.

"Are you invited?"

I nodded again.

Margo turned to Michael. "I suppose you're dining with the Queen, too?"

"I'm not eating. I'm only going along to make sure Mama behaves herself and doesn't steal the silver."

"And who's going to keep an eye on you?" I retorted.

"Kel, I want details. Who's going to be there? What are you wearing?" Margo looked down at her plate. "Who stole my shrimp?"

Paul pointed to the floor where Minx, my calico cat, sat washing her face with her paw.

"I'll put her out." I picked up Minx, cradling her in my arms as we headed for the gallery door. No shrimp smell on her breath. Out of the corner of my eye I spotted Michael wiping crumbs from his mustache.

"Watch out, Margo, someone is tiefin' your food and blaming Minx. Paybacks are hell, guys. No key lime pie for you two." I opened the wrought iron gallery door with my foot and went outside with Minx.

A car pulled into my parking area. Minx jumped out of my arms, darting into the bush.

"Hi, Kel. I thought I'd stop by for a drink." Jerry got out of his car. "Margo said you would be here tonight. Heidi's been in bed all day with the flu, I was bored and decided to go for a drive."

By ourselves we're a healthy lot, but when tourist season comes, it's sick city on St. Chris. Every damned cold and flu bug making the rounds up North finds its way to our shores.

"C'mon in, Jerry. What can I get you? A white-on-white?"

"Sounds good." We entered through the gallery door. "I like what you did in here. Still got your tree up? Heidi made me take ours down on Three Kings' Day. She said it was a fire hazard. But it still had more needles than yours did when you bought it. How much did you pay for that thing?"

"Move over, guys, make some room," I said, heading for the kitchen. "Jerry, pull up a chair."

I brought Jerry his drink and a plate.

"I didn't come for dinner. I had homemade soup with Heidi." He looked at the assortment of shrimp, chicken, steak, mushrooms, and pea pods in individual bowls on the table ready for cooking. "Well, maybe just one shrimp." He snagged one of Margo's red-handled fondue forks, speared a shrimp, and dropped it in the pot. "Where's the sweet-and-sour sauce?"

Margo pointed to a small lotus flower bowl. "Have at it, Jer. Now, as I was saying before"—she paused to make a face at Jerry—"details, Kel. I want details about Miss Maude's dinner for the Queen."

"I know all about that," said Jerry. "I heard Chris talking about it. Miss Maude's known the Queen forever. They went to school together or something."

"Jerry, get your facts straight," said Margo. "Miss Maude's old enough to be the Queen Mum, for Lord's sake."

"Whatever," said Jerry, sipping his drink while the rest of us continued eating. "The point is this: the real reason the Queen is stopping off here, on the way to a tall ships thing in San Juan, is to visit Miss Maude and present her with some sort of an award. Everything else that's planned is window dressing. Chris says the governor isn't very happy about it." He searched the fondue pot for a red-handled fork. "Who stole my shrimp?"

Margo licked her lips and smiled.

# Chapter 4

"MAMA, IT'S THE middle of the night. Where are you going with that hammer?"

"The fairground. Benjamin conned me into working on the homestead house. He wants you there too. Let's get rolling. We're supposed to meet him at eleven and it's now ten-thirty."

Michael looked up from his coffee cup. He was sitting on a bar stool at the tiled table in the center of my kitchen. I'd finished the dinner party cleanup and had a bag of trash ready to drop off at the dump.

"It's Super Bowl Sunday, Mama. Paul and I are watching pregame stuff at Port in a Storm at one."

"You can bug out early from the fairground." I put my arms around Michael. "I never promised you'd show up. I forgot you'd made plans with Paul." Michael and I have a firm rule in our relationship: One never makes plans for the other.

Michael kissed me tasting of French Roast. "Tell you what, Mama. I'm going home to change first, then if I have time, I'll stop at the fairground on the way to Port in a Storm."

"Works for me."

Michael kissed me again, then took off on his Harley. I loaded the trash in my car and headed down the road behind him.

It was a typical St. Chris winter Sunday morning. Temperature edging toward the mid-eighties, easterly trade winds rattling the palm fronds, puffy white clouds drifting in an azure sky. The only thing we needed to make the day absolutely perfect was rain. Winter is our dry season and threats of brush fires are always present.

I drove slowly through Isabeya. Church services had just ended and the streets were momentarily clogged with traffic, but in less than an hour would be deserted. The tourist shops were firmly shuttered; only the pharmacy was open from nine until one, to accommodate readers of Sunday papers. Brunch was served at Dockside's Posh Nosh restaurant from eleven until one, but the Watering Hole was always closed from Saturday afternoon to Monday morning.

Sunday sailors were already at sea; sails of various sizes and configurations tacked back and forth across the horizon. Although the hotel at Harborview was closed for the season because of storm damage and reconstruction, the beach was full of chattering sunbathers and squealing children splashing in sun-dappled wavelets.

I followed the main road out of Isabeya, past the airport turnoff, to the fairground located across from the St. Chris high school, halfway to the west end of the island. The fairground was part of the agricultural station located on the site of Central Factory, a former sugar cane processing plant.

When the Danes bought St. Chris from the French in 1733, St. Chris became Denmark's sugar bowl. The island was surveyed and divided into matriculars of 150 Danish acres each, the size of a working sugar plantation. During the Golden Age of Sugar, each plantation was self-sufficient, processing its own sugar cane in picturesque two-story stone structures that still dot the island like giant thimbles. The machinery that ground the sugar cane was driven first by horse or mule, then by wind, and finally by steam.

The glory days of sugar on St. Chris were over by 1820, but cane continued to be a major crop for another hundred years. On Transfer Day in 1917, no one knew that in three years the passage of the Volstead Act would sound a death knell for the St. Chris economy. By the time Prohibition was repealed in 1933, many of the sugar plantations had been abandoned and sold for back taxes or delinquent mortgages. The few remaining sugar growers consolidated their processing operations into one plant known as Central Factory. When Central Factory shut down for good in the early 1960s, tourism had become the new cash crop.

The homestead program was developed in the 1930s to provide self-sufficiency for the unemployed cane workers. The original homestead homes, built by the homesteaders themselves, were simple two-room wooden structures with lean-to kitchens and outdoor privies. None exist today except in memories and old photographs.

The fairground was deserted except for a few cars in the parking area.

Trevor came bounding up to my car. "Hi, Miss Kelly. We're building a house for the fair. Have you come to help? Did you know this is the fair's twenty-fifth birthday? The theme is 'Back to Our Roots.' I know that because I made a poster for the fair at school. Miss Kelly, listen to this." He paused, thought for a minute, then said haltingly, *"Hvordan har De det?"* He smiled at me, patiently awaiting my response.

"Excuse me?"

"I said 'How are you?' in Danish. Miss Maude is teaching me Danish so I can talk to the Queen."

"Trevor, that's really cool. But I don't know how to answer you."

"I do. You say, *'Tak, godt; og De?'* That means, 'I'm fine, thank you, how are you?' Now you try it."

Trevor and I practiced our Danish as we walked to the homestead house building site.

Hunched over a worktable fashioned from a sheet of plywood resting on sawhorses, Benjamin and his police officers, in their blue St. Chris PD T-shirts, were discussing a set of building plans with a man in a red shirt who looked like a construction foreman.

The man in the red shirt raised his head as we approached and called out, "Hey, Morning Lady, you here to give us a hand?"

"Maubi! I thought you were out of the construction business."

Maubi looked down at his leg, injured in a construction accident that left him with a permanent limp and occasionally dependent on a cane, "I don't climb no more, but I can still drive a nail." He motioned me over to the table. "Check out these plans, Morning Lady."

I looked at the single sheet of yellowed paper, lined with ink faded to sepia.

"This is what my granddaddy use when he build his house. That old wood house gone now, the storms and the termites carry it away, but we still live on the land."

Maubi opened a photo album to proudly display a black and white picture of his grandmother with five children, all dressed in their Sunday best, standing in front of a newly finished homestead house. Seated in an open car in front of them, shaking hands with Maubi's grandfather, was a man with a jaunty grin on his face and a cigarette holder in his hand. I knew I'd seen that grin before.

"Maubi, this is wonderful. When was it taken?"

"Nineteen hundred and thirty-four."

"Who's the man in the car? He looks very familiar."

"That is President Franklin Delano Roosevelt."

I looked again. It really was President Roosevelt, or a very good look-alike.

"The President come to St. Chris for a little visit in 1934, and while he here, he presented a brass plaque to my granddaddy for the best-looking homestead. I got that plaque today in a concrete pillar in front of my own house. You come see it sometime, Morning Lady."

"Me, too?" piped up Trevor. "I want to see it, too. I'll bring my camera and take a picture of it for my scrapbook."

Maubi grinned at Trevor. "Sure, you come too. I'll make some of my special ice cream for you."

"I really like ice cream," said Trevor. "I'm saving all my money to spend at the fair. Are you going to have ice cream at the fair? Last year I had soursop, guavaberry, and mango. My mom gave me a taste of her gooseberry, but I didn't like it. The seeds were too big. I had to spit them out. My mom doesn't like it when I spit."

We were interrupted by the arrival of Chris Edwards, dressed for the links, sporting his shark logo hat. The Government House limo idled in the fairground parking lot.

"Just stopping by on my way to the club. How is everything coming along?" Chris favored us with a pearly smile that made me think of Bobby Darin's rendition of "Mack the Knife." He glanced at the plans on the table, then at the bare building site. "I hope this will be done by fair time. After all, we can't disappoint Her Majesty." He glanced at his watch and flashed another suite. "Can't stay. Running late. Call me at Government House if you need anything. I'm always here to help."

Maubi tracked Chris's departure. "That man always full of talk. But I never see him roll up his sleeves to make a sweat."

# Chapter
## 5

BEFORE YOU COULD say *frikadeller* (fried meatballs) or *fiskefrikadeller* (fried fishballs), Isabeya was firmly in the grip of Danish mania.

When I arrived at the Watering Hole round table for lunch shortly after noon on Monday, Carole shoved a glass in my hand.

"Taste this, Kel. Tell me what you think."

"What is it?"

"A new drink I'm inventing. Taste it." Carole hovered at my side like a sandflea in attack mode, awaiting my response.

I sipped. "Not bad. It's obviously a variation on a theme of Bloody Mary. But what in the hell did you use for booze? It doesn't taste like vodka. Not unless you filtered it through a loaf of rye bread."

"Aquavit. I used aquavit instead of vodka. It's made in Denmark, you know. From potatoes, just like vodka. I'm going to call the drink a Danish Mary. Tell me what it needs."

"A dill pickle."

"Be serious."

"I am being serious. Leave out the Worcestershire sauce." I took another sip. "Add a bit more lime juice." A third sip. "Put in a touch of horseradish." I handed the glass back to Carole. "Garnish it with a pickle spear and you'll have a winner."

"You think so? I'll make you another one. On the house, of course."

The restaurant was full of lunchtime patrons, but I was sitting by myself at the round table. "Where is everyone?"

"Running late, I guess. Jerry and Margo were here an hour ago. I think they're in a powwow at Island Palms." Carole hurried back to the bar.

Abby was the first to join me. "How goes it, Kel?"

"Okay, how's your day?"

"Not bad. But all anyone wants to talk about is the royal visit and how good it will be for the island. I haven't seen so much red and white on Kongens Gade since Christmas."

"Tell me about it. We even started Danish lessons on the air at the station this morning. Learn Danish in thirty days. The Lurpak butter distributor is sponsoring the program."

Carole came back from the bar bearing a frosty mug with a pickle sticking out of the top. "I thought a frosted mug looked better than a glass. Taste this one." She turned to Abby. "You want to try one?"

Abby looked down at the mug over the rim of her sunglasses. "What is it?"

I shoved the untasted drink over to Abby. "You try it, Mikey."

Abby took a small sip, then pushed the drink back at me. "That's really interesting, but I think I'll stick with iced coffee."

Jerry and Margo came out of Island Palms Real Estate deep in conversation. I heard Jerry say to Margo, "Let me know what you decide," before they joined us at the table.

"Carole got you too, Kel? Jerry and I have been tasting those damned drinks all morning. A pickle? Nice touch. Why didn't I think of that." Margo picked up the mug and took a sip, then handed it to Jerry. "This needs more . . . something. I don't know. What do you think, Jerry?"

Jerry drained the mug to the halfway mark. "Worcestershire. It definitely needs a dash of Lea and Perrins. And more Tabasco."

I laughed, told Jerry to finish the drink, and called out to Carole, "I'd like an iced tea, please."

"What's the news at Government House this morning, Jer?" asked Abby.

"I wasn't there much, but the phones were ringing off the hook. Everyone wants to get on the invitation list for the Queen's lunch and the afternoon garden party." Jerry looked around to see who was lunching at the Watering Hole, waved at a few people, then lowered his voice. "The lunch is restricted to senators and high government officials, but I think I can get you all on the garden party list. I'll put in a word with Chris when I see him. His secretary said he was holed up in conference with the governor most of the morning."

"Jerry, how long are you going to milk that Disaster Relief job at Government House?" I said. "Gilda is practically ancient history."

"I still have reports to write," said Jerry solemnly. "But I need to review the final assessment data with the governor and that could take a while. Chris says the guv may not be available until after the royal visit." Jerry shrugged and got up to head to the bar for a drink refill.

I smiled and turned to Margo. "How's the real estate biz today?"

"Picking up. But it's the same old story. The sellers want the moon, even for properties with storm damage, and the buyers want bargains. You haven't changed your mind?"

"Get off it, Margo. I'm not selling my house."

Abby looked up from the lunch menu. "Kel, are you moving?"

"No way. Margo, where did you get this crazy idea about selling my house?"

"It's kind of small for two people, and I thought . . ."

"Thought what?"

"You and Michael might need more room."

"Ixnay, sweetie. Unless you know something I don't know."

"Well, you two have been together for what? A year now?"

"That doesn't mean you should be getting any ideas," I said. "I'm happy with things just the way they are."

"Now that you own WBZE, how does Michael like working for the boss?" asked Abby.

"He seems okay with it. We're seldom there at the same time. We went back to twenty-four/seven when we got power restored and curfew was lifted. He starts at ten P.M. and signs off when I sign on at six A.M. We don't see each other much during the week, but we never did. He finally got his place on the west end rebuilt, so we're back to where we were before the storm. It works for me." I directed my last remarks to Margo. "Read my lips, sweetie. I am not, repeat, am not, interested in selling my house."

"I get the message, Kel."

"Good. Tell you what, because you're so understanding, I'll buy your lunch today. What's on the menu?"

Abby began to laugh. "Who ever heard of Danish pizza? Listen to this. 'Individual pizzas, topped with your choice of herring and red cabbage or ham and pickled beets.' Gag me with a brick. When did the Watering Hole chef become Denmark's answer to Wolfgang Puck? I'm going to have a good old American cheeseburger, medium-rare."

Carole stood by ready to take our orders. "Would you like a slice of Jarlsberg cheese on that burger?" she asked brightly. "It's Danish, you know."

Abby motioned to Carole to come closer, then whispered in her ear.

"Jarlsberg is made in Norway? Are you sure?" asked Carole.

Abby nodded.

"Bummer," said Carole, crestfallen but recovering quickly. "Well, then, how about Danish blue cheese?"

Abby groaned and rolled her eyes, throwing up her hands in surrender to Carole's Danish mania.

Carole smiled as she went to the kitchen to place our orders.

# Chapter

# 6

AFTER LUNCH I went back to WBZE to catch up on paperwork and think about hiring someone for a receptionist position.

Michael wasn't the only change in my life in the past year. I'd also gone from being strictly WBZE's weekday morning deejay, to morning deejay and general manager, and now I was the morning deejay, general manager, and *capo di capo*. The boss of bosses. My life had been a lot simpler when I wore only one hat and someone else had the money worries. Now that I owned the station free and clear, I had a weekly payroll to meet and advertisers to woo.

Before Mrs. H, WBZE's previous owner, skipped off on her six-month 'round-the-world cruise, her granddaughter Emily had been our receptionist. A sweet girl, although perhaps not the brightest bulb in the chandelier and possessed of a fondness for chewing gum that bordered on a bovine obsession, Emily was dedicated, even if she occasionally filed classical composers by first names rather than last. But Emily was history after Gilda. She was currently attending junior college in Florida and spending her holidays in Italy with her grandmother.

I dreaded having to hire and train someone new.

The phone rang. I answered with our standard greeting, "WBZE, the breath of fresh music in the Caribbean."

"Hey, Kel. Where are you?"

"Margo, you idiot, I'm at the station. You called me."

"Blame it on speed dial. I couldn't remember if I punched the station or your home number. What are you doing?"

"Paperwork. Bor-ring."

"Same here. I'm going to shut up shop and go home. Why don't you come over to Sea Breezes, we'll have a drink at Port in a Storm. Something without aquavit in it."

"Amen, sister. See you in thirty at the bar."

The beach at Sea Breezes, the condo complex west of Isabeya where Margo and Paul lived, was filled with snowbirds, condo owners who showed up during the Christmas holidays and left after Easter to go back to homes in the winter-chilled North. I waved to several I knew as I headed for the bar.

Mitch was racking clean glasses. "Hi, Kelly. What'll it be? We've got a special on Tuborg. Denmark's finest. The Carlsberg shipment will be here tomorrow. Have you ever had a Carlsberg Elephant? Packs quite a wallop."

Danish mania had hit Port in a Storm.

"You talked me into a Tuborg. With a glass of ice, please."

"You want a squeeze of lime in that? One of the snow-birds told me it's the latest thing."

"Is scurvy going around these days?"

Mitch winked.

"I'll pass on the lime."

Margo breezed in a few minutes later, dressed in a bathing suit and sarong cover-up. "Too bad you didn't bring a suit, we could go for a swim. What are you drinking?"

"Tuborg. Mitch is running a special."

"Did you tell him about the Danish pizza?"

I shook my head.

"I'll try a Tuborg," Margo said to Mitch. "Wait until I tell you what was on the menu at the Watering Hole today."

I sipped my beer while Margo chatted with Mitch. When other customers clamored for his attention, she turned to me. "Let's go outside and grab a couple of sand chairs. I need your advice."

We settled ourselves on the sand in the shade of a coconut palm. The fronds swished slowly above our heads.

"What's up, sweetie?" I said.

"Jerry had a call from Pete Sunday afternoon. Pete wants us to buy him out."

Margo, Jerry, and Pete my ex-husband now married to Angie and the proud parents of a five-month-old baby boy were partners in Island Palms Real Estate.

"What brought this on?"

"Hang on, Kel, I'm going to get us two more beers. Then I've got something to tell you."

I wriggled my toes in the warm sand and gazed at the whitecap-flecked azure sea until Margo returned.

"Mitch said these are on the house. Stop back at the bar before you leave, he wants to go over some new ad copy with you."

"What do you want to tell me?"

"Kel, if you ever repeat any of this, I'll deny I ever said it." Margo caught the look on my face. "I know, I know. We've been friends forever, but I had to say it anyway. This really isn't my news to tell."

We clinked beer bottles to seal the pact.

"Kel, Pete and Angie are having a real hard time financially. Angie hasn't worked in almost a year, I can't remember when Pete last had a big real estate sale. That's why we never see him at the round table anymore. He can't afford it."

"I had no idea. When Pete and I split, he was the one with money. He made megabucks in Chicago as a stockbroker. I wonder where it all went."

"That was then, Kel. Maybe his investments went sour. Who knows? And there's more." Margo paused for a swallow of beer. "Angie's pregnant. Again."

"Why am I not surprised?" I said, thinking to myself that Pete never could keep his pants zipped, even when we were still married and he developed a roving eye to go with his Robert Redford smile. "So Pete wants out of real estate. What's he going to do?"

"Work for Angie's father. The family owns Island Lumber, you know."

"If I knew that, I forgot it. I have a hard time picturing Pete working in a lumberyard. When we were married, his idea of home repair was picking up the phone to call a handyman. That's when I started learning how to do stuff around the house." I smiled. "I remember the first time I installed a new light switch. I was scared to death I was going to electrocute myself. Talk about 'Hey there, you with the sweat on your palms.' Best headline Stan Freberg ever wrote."

"Kel, who in the hell is Stan Freberg?"

"Sweetie, were you raised in a cave hidden deep in the forest? Stan Freberg did those really great satirical ad campaigns for Chung King, Jeno's Pizza Rolls, Heinz Soup. Remember Ann Miller dancing on the soup can? The 'sweat on your palms' bit was a headline from a print ad for Pacific Airlines."

"Kel, you have a mind full of trivia."

"Never mind, sweetie. Let's get back to your problem with the buyout."

"Right. According to our partnership agreement, the remaining partners have the first option to buy out another partner. I thought Jerry and I would go fifty-fifty on Pete's share, but Jerry's not interested. He's so busy sucking up at Government House, he hardly spends any time at Island Palms."

"And this surprises you? Before Gilda, Jerry seemed to divide his time between the round table and the golf course."

"I know." Margo sighed. "I love Jerry like a brother, but he sure can be a pain in the butt. I guess I'll have to buy out Pete on my own. There go my savings." She sighed again. "And I'll also be stuck with two-thirds of the monthly overhead."

"Look at the bright side, you'll also reap two-thirds of the profits."

"If there are any. I'll have to get in gear and sell some real estate. If you know anyone who's looking, send them to me."

"I always do."

"You're a pal, Kel. Did you ever think we would end up being moguls?"

I shook my head. "There are times I wonder if buying WBZE was my smartest move."

"Buyer's remorse?"

"Not really. I liked working with Mrs. H, but when she said she wanted to sell, I knew I'd be happier working for myself than someone I didn't know."

"So what's the problem?"

"I need office help. I've been taking paperwork home at night. I haven't had any front office staff since Emily left."

"Forgive me for saying this. But losing Emily was no loss. She was sweet, but a major flake."

"Come on, she wasn't that bad."

"Kel, you told me yourself she couldn't file worth spit. Every time I called you, she cracked her gum in my ear. Is that really the image you want for WBZE?"

"Sweetie, WQXR we're not. This isn't the Big Apple. We're a small tropical island radio station."

"You still could use some smarts at the front desk. You can't do everything. I bet you can find someone who can pronounce Shostakovich."

"Those Russian names are tricky." Naming classical composers had not been Emily's strong suit.

"Kel, forget the Russians. Emily had trouble with Beethoven and Mozart and Handel."

"If you hear of anyone who's looking, let me know."

We ended the first meeting of the St. Chris Business Women's Association by adjourning to the bar.

# Chapter 7

FRIDAY AFTERNOON FOUND me in Miss Maude's kitchen watching Miss Lucinda labor over a hot stove.

"Keep stirring, Lucy," said Miss Maude. "If you stop, it'll get lumpy and the entire batch will be ruined."

Miss Lucinda dropped the wooden spoon in the kettle and walked away from the stove, her face set in a pout. "When my husband was alive, I never had to cook."

I grabbed the spoon and began stirring vigorously. "It's okay, Miss Maude, I'll take over for a while."

"Lucy, why don't you take the tea tray out to the gallery where it's cooler. There's a fresh batch of cookies in a tin in the pantry."

Miss Lucinda brightened at the mention of cookies and set off for the gallery with a smile and a light step. I noticed she was wearing the same new shoes she'd worn the previous Saturday.

I continued stirring, watching the tapioca begin to turn from opaque to crystal clear. We were making red grout, or *rødgrød* as the Danes called it, for Miss Maude's Saturday night dress rehearsal of the upcoming dinner for the Queen.

Miss Maude leaned over my shoulder to peer in the kettle. "That looks very nice, Kelly. Keep stirring. You might want to turn down the flame a bit." She lowered her voice to add, "I'm afraid Lucy is being a bit peevish. This is not one of her better days."

I nodded and continued stirring. In the five months since Hurricane Gilda, Miss Lucinda had become increasingly moody and talked more and more of the past when, as the island rumor mill was fond of regaling newcomers in excited whispers, she had a brief romantic interlude with the Prince of Wales. Not Charles, the current Prince of Wales, but the one who became King Edward the Eighth and abdicated to marry "that Baltimore trollop," as Miss Lucinda often described Wallis Simpson. Whether the rumor was true or not, no one knew for sure. But we all indulged Miss Lucinda and openly admired the Art Deco platinum and diamond watch she wore on her left wrist, a gift, she said, from her David.

For protection from Hurricane Gilda, Miss Lucinda had locked herself in a linen closet and languished there for thirty-six hours, forgetting she had the key to the closet tucked in her pocket. By the time she was discovered, she was very dehydrated and quite delirious. After three weeks in the hospital, she was released into Miss Maude's care. Although Miss Lucinda continued to live in her own home, waited on hand and foot by her housekeeper, I thought the strain of looking out for her friend was wearing on Miss Maude, but I refrained from comment.

"What's the next step?" I asked, still stirring the tapioca.

"We will add the raisins and prunes, with a pinch of salt, and stir over low heat for five more minutes. Then we'll stir in the red food coloring. In the old days we used stewed prickly pear juice for color. Then we'll pour it into a mold to chill until we're ready to serve it tomorrow night with vanilla-flavored sweet cream sauce. On a Danish dessert menu it's listed as *rødgrød med fløde*."

"I can't wait for the Ag Fair," I said. "I love the food." Each year my first stop at the fair was the food building, where the church ladies and various St. Chris service groups set up booths selling locally made treats. I always started with a paper cup full of ginger beer or maubi, then worked my way from booth to booth eating pates, kallaloo, and johnnycakes, ending up outside at Maubi's van for homemade coconut ice cream.

"If you took the time, you could be making these same things in your own kitchen."

"Miss Maude, I gave up real cooking with the storm. All those months of canned tuna killed my appetite. Now I don't cook anything that takes longer to prepare than it does to eat. I can't believe that when I lived in Chicago, I used to spend eight hours in the kitchen following every step of Julia Child's recipe for beef bourguignonne. That's when I was feeling flush. When I was broke, it was ten-minute dollar stew."

Miss Maude said with an inquiring look, "I don't believe I've ever heard of dollar stew."

"It was a silly thing I concocted a long time ago when food prices were much cheaper. Fifty cents' worth of ground beef, a chopped-up onion, a diced potato, and three small cans of vegetables." I didn't tell Miss Maude that when I was really broke, I ate uncooked hot dogs dipped in mustard. But only if hot dogs were on special that week.

"You modern working women," said Miss Maude with a smile. "Amelia thinks the same way you do. In my day, if we didn't cook, we didn't eat. The only canned goods we had were those we put up ourselves."

"Next you'll be telling me stories of chopping wood in a raging blizzard."

"Don't be smart with me, young lady." There was a twinkle in Miss Maude's eyes as she glanced in the kettle. "Keep stirring. Two more minutes. I'll get the mold ready."

I stirred until I thought my arm would drop off, while mentally applauding frozen food and microwaves. While we were cleaning up the kitchen, I asked, "What else is on the menu?"

"Chilled cucumber soup for the first course, then baked fish and asparagus pudding for the main course. My mother brought the asparagus pudding recipe with her from Denmark. I think of her every time I prepare it. There will be, of course, red grout for dessert."

"It all sounds delicious. Is there anything else I can do?"

"Nothing at all, dear. Thank you for all your help. I'll see you and Michael tomorrow night at seven." She pressed a small container of red grout in my hand. "Enjoy this with your dinner tonight. If you don't want to make vanilla cream sauce, you can top it with whipped cream or a small scoop of vanilla ice cream."

Michael and I showed up at the appointed hour the following evening dressed for the occasion, but saving our formal wear for the night when the Queen would be present. For the Queen I'd even wear pantyhose and closed high-heeled shoes.

Miss Maude's dining table was beautifully set for nine—the governor, Queen Margrethe and Prince Henrik would fill the remaining three places the night of the official dinner—with a white linen cloth and her best china, crystal, and silver. In the center of the table was a bowl of freshly cut red, orange, and peach hibiscus; flanked on either side by forest green candles in spotless glass hurricane globes. Overhead a ceiling fan twirled lazily on low.

We found the rest of the party on the back gallery enjoying cocktails, serenaded by twittering birds, croaking frogs, and rasping crickets. Fireflies, nature's twinkie lights, blipped slowly in and out of the fruit trees bordering the property. Miss Maude and Miss Lucinda, looking very elegant in below-the-knee silk print dresses, were seated in comfortable wicker armchairs. Camille was chatting with Amelia and her husband, while Benjamin tended bar. Camille, Amelia, and I had all chosen to wear long skirts with sandals. Benjamin and Amelia's husband were dressed in slacks and guyaberra shirts made of handkerchief-fine cotton, enhanced with color-on-color embroidery, standard St. Chris evening attire. Jackets and ties being reserved for funerals or going to court. Michael had abandoned his luridly flowered workweek aloha shirts for a classic white Oxford cloth button-down. We were a spiffy-looking group.

"When Chris arrives, we'll move to the dining room," said Miss Maude on her way to the kitchen.

I followed behind her. "Is there anything I can do to help you?"

The kitchen was full of mouth-watering smells. Miss Maude opened the oven to check on the fish, caught from the Caribbean Sea that very afternoon, baking in butter and lime juice, topped with sliced onions, and generously seasoned with herbs from her own garden. On top of the stove the asparagus pudding was steaming in boiling water.

"If you would take this platter out to the gallery, I can manage everything else. The evening Queen Margrethe and Prince Henrik are here, Amelia's daughters will help serve dinner."

I took the plate containing curry dip with tiny johnnycakes and assorted vegetables out to the gallery.

Miss Lucinda took one look at the platter and put her free hand back in her lap. "Tell Maude I want some of those cheese things." She motioned to Benjamin for a refill on her drink.

I walked over to Michael, who slid his arm around my waist. "What is Miss Lucinda drinking?" I whispered in his ear.

"I don't know, Mama, but it's not her first," he whispered back. "Could be Tanqueray on the rocks. She looks like a gin hound." In a normal tone he said, "What can I get for you? Gin and tonic?"

"What are you having?"

"Scotch rocks. There isn't any Heineken."

"I'll have club soda with lime. I think there's going to be wine with dinner and I'm the designated driver tonight."

Michael grinned, gave me a thumbs-up, and headed for the bar.

I went to join Camille and Amelia.

"Kelly, I don't think you've met my husband Frederik," Amelia said. "Freddy, this is Granny Maude's dear friend Kelly." We shook hands and engaged in the usual "nice to meet you at last" small talk.

Further conversation was interrupted by the arrival of Chris Edwards. Miss Maude hurried out from the kitchen to greet him. He handed her a bottle of wine and they headed to the kitchen to put it on ice.

"Kelly, did you get a look at the label on that bottle?" asked Camille. "I could feed my family for a week on the price of that one bottle."

"I bet he nicked it from the guv's wine cellar," I said.

Camille raised her cocktail glass to her mouth to cover her smile.

The two-days-past-full moon was peeping dusky orange over the east end hills when Miss Maude came out to the gallery to ask us all to be seated at the dining table. Benjamin helped Miss Lucinda out of her chair and she promptly detoured to the bar in quick, short steps to top off her glass.

Miss Maude sat at the head of the table with Chris on her left, Miss Lucinda on her right; Amelia was next to Chris, followed by Benjamin then me. Freddy sat next to Miss Lucinda followed by Camille and Michael.

When the soup course was cleared, Miss Maude served the baked fish and asparagus pudding. The dinner was as delicious as anticipated and everyone had second servings.

Miss Maude suggested we retire to the back gallery for coffee and red grout with vanilla cream sauce. It was then that Chris finally served the bottle of wine he'd brought. "Champagne is much better with dessert than the main course," he said.

Before we picked up our dessert spoons, Chris raised his wineglass. "I wish to make a toast to our hostess for this splendid dinner, which I know will be a highlight of the Queen's visit. To you, Maude."

We all raised our glasses and sipped the wine. Miss Lucinda dutifully raised her glass but left it untasted, muttering "Champagne makes me windy," and headed to the bar to refresh her drink. I thought the wine tasted a little flat, but what did I know about really good and very expensive champagne? I usually spring for something in the five-dollar-a-bottle range with a plastic cork, the sweeter the wine the better. Anything brut or extra brut tends to grab my throat glands like a childhood case of the mumps. A bit of trivia I was wise enough to keep to myself.

By ten o'clock we were thanking our hostess for a wonderful evening.

Michael and I drove slowly through Isabeya, both of us too stuffed from dinner to say very much. The Kongens

Gade bars were in full-tilt Saturday night boogie, spilling light, music, and patrons onto the narrow street. We were on the east end road five minutes away from my house when Michael suddenly said, "Pedal to the metal, Mama, or stop here and let me out now. I'm going to be sick."

# Chapter
# 8

WE BARELY MADE it to my house. Michael never made it inside. I opened the kitchen door and ran to the loo, getting there just in time. Then it was Michael's turn. It was what I would indelicately call an "all systems go" flu bug.

My water pump switched on and off for a good half hour while we used a month's worth of water for flushing. If we didn't get rain soon, I'd have to brush up on my rain dance or buy water. The east end was so dry that the croton leaves in my front yard were shriveling in the sun. The desiccated seedpods of the Mother Tongue trees on the hillside behind the house rattled in the easterly trade winds like castanets.

"Mama, I ache like hell and I can't get warm. My head hurts."

"Crawl in bed, Michael. I'll be there as soon as I find an extra blanket."

I already had a winter comforter on my king-sized bed—when the temperature gets down to sixty-eight at night, it feels damned nippy to those of us who live here year 'round—and topped it with a cozy fleece blanket. We needed warmth, not weight. I went to the kitchen for some ginger ale and poured each of us a glass, carrying it back to bed with Imodium and Tylenol for two.

We slept fitfully, each of us making several trips to the john. Perhaps Margo was right; maybe I did need a bigger house. At least one with two bathrooms.

We still felt like hell Sunday morning. I turned off the phone, let the machine pick up any messages, closed all the drapes, fed Minx and let her out, then crawled back into bed.

In a strange way it was one of the nicest and most relaxing days Michael and I'd spent together in a long time. We took turns getting more ginger ale, and slept the day away curled next to each other like kittens in a box.

We were roused from sleep late Sunday afternoon by Minx's yowling at the kitchen door.

"Mama, you stay in bed. I'll feed the feline."

"How are you feeling?"

"Like death warmed over, but I'll live. I wish I had the number of the truck that hit me."

I turned over and went back to sleep. I woke again early evening to find Michael dozing next to me and Minx curled in a ball at our feet.

"What time is it, Mama?"

"Eight o'clock."

"Morning or night?"

"It's night, Michael. The sun would be up if it were morning."

I struggled out of bed and put on a thick terry cloth robe. "Could you handle some soup?"

"As long as it doesn't have any garlic in it. I can't get that taste out of my mouth." Michael made a face that would have scared off any vampire within miles. "I feel like gargling with Clorox."

"Try baking soda. There's a box in the medicine cabinet. Mix a couple of tablespoons with half a glass of warm water. How about some chicken noodle soup, or chicken and stars?"

"Okay with me. Is there any more ginger ale?"

I brought mugs of hot soup and a big bottle of ginger ale back to bed. Then I went to check the answering machine while my soup cooled.

There were brief messages from Camille, Amelia, and Miss Maude. Everyone was sick. Miss Maude sounded like she'd been crying.

I took the phone back to bed and called Camille.

Trevor answered the phone on the first ring. "My parents can't talk to you now, Miss Kelly, they have the flu and they're sleeping."

"Tell them I called. I have the flu, too. So does Michael."

"Do you want me to come over on my bike and make you some soup?"

"It's sweet of you to offer, Trevor, but no thank you. I just made some. Tell your parents I'll talk to them tomorrow."

I got up at four-thirty Monday morning and went to work as usual, feeling like something Minx had dragged home from the bush, leaving Michael tucked in bed with Minx at his side.

Benjamin called me at the station midmorning. "How are you feeling, Kelly?"

"Better. How about you and Camille?"

"We're better too. So are Amelia and Freddy."

"That was some flu bug."

"I don't think we had the flu. I think it was fish poisoning."

"Benjamin, you've got to be kidding. That fish tasted just fine."

"It doesn't have to taste bad to give you ciguatera."

"I've never had it, I wouldn't know."

"I haven't had it either. But I'm going to do some checking and I'll let you know."

"How's Miss Maude? She left a message on my answering machine yesterday. She sounded like she'd been crying."

"She was sick, too, Kelly. She's mortified that we all were ill. All she could say to me was, 'What if the Queen had been here?' She thinks she should cancel the royal dinner."

"Oh, Benjamin. Poor Miss Maude. She is so looking forward to the royal visit. She's the main reason they're coming to St. Chris. The Queen and Prince have to eat somewhere. Tell Miss Maude to change the menu and serve something else . . . like roast beef or turkey with all the trimmings. Talk to her."

"I'll try, but you know Miss Maude."

"You know her better than I do, Benjamin. She was your teacher." Benjamin had been in the last class Miss Maude taught in the school on Danish Hill before her retirement.

Benjamin chuckled. "When Miss Maude makes up her mind about something, she sticks to it. Camille and Amelia are going over to see her this afternoon after school." Amelia was the principal of the St. Chris high school, Camille was her assistant.

"I have to go home and check on Michael when I'm off the air at noon. I'll call Miss Maude later."

"I'll call you if I find out anything."

After Benjamin hung up, I immediately dialed Miss Maude's number. If she was home, she wasn't answering the phone.

# Chapter
# 9

MICHAEL AND MINX were still sleeping soundly when I walked through the kitchen door shortly after twelve. I had driven straight home from the station. No passing go, no collecting $200, no stopping for lunch at the Watering Hole.

I tiptoed to my bookshelves and assumed the scanning position: semicrouch, head cocked right, eyes vertical, moving slowly backward in baby steps.

"Mama, what in the hell are you doing? You look like a crazed Quasimodo."

Startled, I looked up to see Michael lying in bed, his head propped on his right hand, watching me with an amused look on his face. Minx had her left rear leg high in the air and was busy bathing. I promptly lost my balance and fell on my tush on the hard terrazzo floor. Michael laughed. Minx hopped off the bed and padded over to me, to rub her face against my arm.

"If I'm Quasimodo, that makes you Frollo," I said, picking up Minx and rubbing her tummy. Minx purred. I slowly stroked her throat with the back of my hand to feel the vibrations. Minx wriggled out of my arms, heading for her food dish in the kitchen. A cat with her priorities always in order.

"Bag the short jokes, Mama. I always wanted to be Esmeralda." Michael stretched and yawned.

"I'll remind you of that next Halloween. How are you feeling?"

"I'll show you." Michael leapt out of bed and came over to where I sat on the floor. He bent down for a kiss.

I held up my hand. "Bat breath. Go brush your teeth first."

He grinned and headed for the loo. "I'm going to take a shower."

I turned back to the bookshelves, spotted the book I was looking for, and pulled it from the shelf. I executed a no-hands cross-legged ascent from the floor, pleased that I was still limber enough to do it, but mildly disappointed that there were no witnesses to applaud. I placed the book on the coffee table, then went for Minx's snack jar on the kitchen counter. I dropped a handful of Haute Feline kitty snacks into her bowl. In less than thirty seconds the bowl was once again empty.

Michael emerged from the shower with a towel wrapped around his waist, and walked over to the living room couch, where I was curled up, reading intently. He lifted the book to look at the cover. "Poison? You're reading a book about poison?" A low whistle escaped his lips. "What gives, Mama? Am I safe in the same room with you?"

"Chill out, Michael." I motioned to him to sit down. "I'm reading about ciguatera. Benjamin called me at the station this morning. He thinks we all had fish poisoning. Listen to this."

Michael reached for my hand to pull me from the couch. "Let's read in bed."

An hour later we returned to the subject of ciguatera.

"Read me that bit again, Mama."

"Which bit?"

"The symptoms."

I found my place in the book. "Symptoms are usually evident within a few hours of eating a contaminated fish and may include: numbness and/or tingling of the lips and extremities; itching, trembling, weakness, aching muscles, joints, and teeth; reduced reflexes and the reversal of the sense of hot and cold. Some of these symptoms may persist for months or years. The vomiting, diarrhea, and abdominal pains appear early and usually resolve themselves within twenty-four hours."

"That doesn't sound much different from ordinary flu. I didn't have any of the numbness, did you?"

I shook my head. "Close your eyes, Michael. I want to try something. No fair peeking." When his eyes were shut, I slipped an ice cube out of my glass and held it against his bare back.

"Yow! Mama, that's cold!"

"See? You can feel the difference between cold and hot."

"What does that prove?"

"I don't know. Except maybe it wasn't fish poisoning after all."

"I don't care what it was, I don't want it again." He pulled me close to him. "Let's catch some z's. The best cure for anything is lots of bed rest."

We never did get around to lunch, and dinner consisted of scrambled eggs and dry toast before Michael had to leave for his shift at WBZE. I walked with him to the kitchen door, where we stood with our arms wrapped around each other.

"You know, Mama, these past two days have been the best time we've had since the storm. We should get sick together more often." He kissed me with a passion that left me feeling tingles in my extremities, having nothing whatsoever to do with tainted fish. He cupped his hand under my chin. "Keep your radio tuned to WBZE and try to hang in until ten-fifteen. The first song tonight is for you."

I fell asleep at ten-twenty humming "Come Rain or Come Shine."

# Chapter
# 10

"KEL, WE MISSED you at lunch yesterday," said Margo. "Where were you?"

"I went home to check on Michael. We both had a touch of flu over the weekend."

"That's not what I heard," said Jerry. "Chris was sick for two days and says it was fish poisoning. He's looking to sue someone."

"You can't be serious. Who's he going to sue? The dead fish? I don't think so."

"Fish poisoning? I hear that's awful," said Margo. "Do you know it never goes away? You can never eat seafood again. And you're not supposed to touch alcohol for at least six months. I think I'd rather die than not have lobster. How sick were you?"

"Margo, it felt like a flu bug. And I think that's exactly what it was."

"Can we talk about something else?" said Abby. "I want to enjoy my lunch."

"What's today's special?" asked Margo. "Oh, Kel. Wait

until I tell you what you missed yesterday. Danish enchiladas."

"You're putting me on," I said.

Margo looked at Abby for confirmation.

Abby nodded. "She's right, Kel."

"Do tell," I said. "Is anyone making a list of this stuff? We could come up with a Watering Hole cookbook."

"Like the *One Hundred Ways to Use Canned Tuna* recipe book you created as a WBZE Christmas giveaway?" said Margo. "Who was the idiot who submitted: 'Canned tuna makes a good doorstop'?"

"That was my idea," said Jerry, sounding very pleased with himself. "But you need a giant economy-size can to really make it work."

"I should have known it was you," Margo muttered in Jerry's direction.

"Who's going to tell me about Danish enchiladas?" I asked.

Margo took center stage. "Beef or chicken, and the usual refried beans, lettuce, onion, tomatoes, topped with grated cheese and sour cream. But here's the kicker. Instead of tortillas? What was it, Abby? Something made with mashed potatoes. But pressed real thin, like a soft tortilla."

"It's called *lefse* in Norway," said Jerry. "It's very good spread with lots of butter or cream cheese. They sometimes stock it at Soup to Nuts."

"Really? I'll have to check it out." Soup to Nuts was a gourmet deli on the east end of Isabeya and one of my biggest advertisers. I turned to Margo. "How were the enchiladas?"

"Good. But messy. I tried picking one up, and it fell apart in my hand. I used a fork after that."

Abby smiled. "Margo, we can dress you up, but we

can't take you out. I think you two might want to take a pass on today's offering."

"What is it?"

Abby read from the menu. "Danish pasta: linguini with *frikadeller* or white herring sauce."

"I pass," I said.

"Ditto," said Margo, looking down at her white shirt and shorts. "Jerry, if you order the special, you'd better move to a table for one. And ask Carole for a bib."

After lunch I strolled along the waterfront boardwalk, passing Dockside on my way to the post office. The ten-passenger ferry filled with chattering tourists carrying beach bags and towels, was just leaving the dock for the brief trip over to Harborview.

Victoria, Dockside's owner, was standing in the court-yard that housed the Lower Deck restaurant, conferring with one of her staff. When she spotted me, she waved and motioned me over.

"Have you time for a drink?" she asked.

"Sure, Vic, but I'd better make it an iced tea."

"Not under the weather, are you?"

"I had a touch of flu over the weekend."

"Were you at the same Saturday evening dinner party with Christopher Edwards? I was supposed to meet with him this morning, but he canceled. He's telling everyone he was poisoned by bad fish served at Miss Maude's house."

Victoria and I walked up the outside staircase to the second floor, where her office, the hotel reception area, and Dockside's Posh Nosh restaurant were located. The Posh Nosh bartender poured us each an iced tea, garnished with a wedge of key lime and a sprig of spearmint, and we went to sit at a small table in the bar area overlooking the harbor.

"Vic, I wish Chris would shut up about being poisoned

by bad fish. I'm tempted to call the guv and ask him to tell Chris to lay off."

"Best of British luck, ducky. Chris protects the governor like a lioness with a baby cub. The only way you can get to the governor is through Chris. And you get to Chris through his secretary. There are more fences at Government House than the one you see on Kongens Gade."

"Vic, Miss Maude is devastated. For all I know, it could have been the flu. The fish tasted fine. It was so good everyone at the table had second servings. Even Chris."

"Fish can be very tricky. I'm most particular about the fish served in my restaurants. What kind was it? That's important. Not all fish are susceptible to ciguatera. Only scavengers like barracuda and red snapper whose food chain includes bottom-dwelling species. Tuna and dolphin are perfectly safe."

I threw up my hands and shrugged. "I don't know what kind it was, Vic. To me, unless it's shrimp or lobster, it all tastes the same. Miss Maude said it was fresh, caught that very afternoon. I've been trying to reach her for the past two days, but she doesn't answer her phone."

Victoria shook her head. "The poor woman. Miss Maude's devoted her life to St. Chris. This should be a happy time for her. I'll pay her a visit. I need to confer with her about the royal luncheon. We're doing the catering for Government House. Imagine it, Kelly. The Queen is coming here. It will be so good for the island. I'm booked solid for the next six weeks." Victoria sighed happily, as awestruck as a kid over a rock star. "I couldn't be more thrilled than if it were Queen Elizabeth herself. Why, when I was a girl growing up in Kent..." She paused to look out the open jalousie windows overlooking the harbor and the east end. "Good heavens."

I followed Victoria's gaze. "Oh, my God." Thick dark smoke was billowing high in the air on the east end.

Where there's smoke in St. Chris in February, there's a brush fire yearning to rage out of control. "Vic, thanks for the tea. I've got to get home." As I ran down the Dockside staircase, I heard the fire truck sirens screaming down Kongens Gade heading for the east end.

# Chapter
# 11

GETTING HOME THROUGH the fire was like riding shotgun with Scarlett and Rhett during the burning of Atlanta in *Gone With the Wind*.

The brushfire blazed on both sides of the east end straightaway a mile before the turnoff to my house. The same area where Michael had said to me three nights earlier: "Pedal to the metal, Mama."

Fire trucks were positioned on both sides of the road. I recognized the police officer directing traffic from the homestead house building crew. He motioned to me to stop. "Where you heading, Kelly?"

"Hey, Alphonso. I'm trying to get home. I live at Goat Hill."

"I'll let you pass. Back up, turn around in the clearing back there, go back about fifty feet, do a U, then floor it. Don't slow down until you're safely past the fire zone." He slapped the top of my car with his palm and called "Car coming through" into his bullhorn.

"Come on, baby, you can do this." I patted my car's

dashboard as I turned around. I was still driving my storm-battered eleven-year-old Japanese hatchback, a top contender for the "It's ugly but it gets you there" award and an ongoing object of Margo's derision. I recalled our last conversation on the subject.

"Kel, I know how frugal you are. But why are you still driving that wreck? You can afford a new car. Treat yourself."

"Have you checked new car prices recently? I was in sticker shock."

"Let WBZE buy you a company car. You can depreciate it as a corporate asset."

"What would the rest of my crew think? They work their buns off to make the station a success and I blow the profits on a new car? I don't think so. It may be legal, but morale-wise it's a bummer. Mrs. H never did that."

"Kel, Mrs. H drove a Mercedes."

"Yes, but she paid for it herself."

Margo reluctantly dropped the subject.

I gripped the steering wheel with my left hand, my right resting on the gear shift; right foot on the gas, left on the clutch. I took a deep breath while the little voice in my head called out, "Gentlemen, start your engines."

Car in first, ease off the clutch, down on the gas.

Heading toward the fire zone.

Foot on the clutch, shift into second, then third.

Snap, crackle, pop. An explosion of glass from a discarded beer bottle.

My eyes began tearing from the smoke. No time to do anything but blink the tears away and keep my eyes firmly fixed on the road ahead of me.

Walls of fire on either side. I felt the shimmering heat through the open car windows, smelled burning grass and tan-tan. Please God, I whispered, don't let me stall out now.

Foot on the clutch, smooth shift into fourth. Ease off
the clutch and floor it. Pedal to the metal. Those three
little cylinders under the hood were pumping out power
for all they were worth. I felt like I was behind the wheel
of *The Little Engine That Could.*

Talk about your "Hey there, you with the sweat on your
palms" moment. I never slowed down or drew a deep
breath until I reached the turnoff leading toward my driveway.

When I pulled into my parking area, I barely had
enough energy left to turn off the ignition and set the
parking brake. And pat the dashboard in gratitude. Good
car.

Then I remembered Top Banana, my bright yellow
kayak, chained to a palm tree at the cove not far from my
home. The easterly trade winds would drive the present
fire west, away from my house, but who knew when another would start? Or where?

I ran inside, quickly changed clothes, and grabbed my
kayak paddle, then drove down to the beach.

Top Banana was full of sand and age-stained orange
seagrape leaves. I dragged the boat to the ocean to clean
it off before loading it onto my car.

The ocean was so calm, so inviting, I couldn't resist its
siren song. "Out to the reef cut and back, twenty minutes
max," I told myself as I shoved off and began paddling.

The sea bed was slowly regenerating after Gilda. Newly
grown grasses undulated in the westerly flowing current,
sheltering the tiny blue and yellow fish I loved to watch.
I paddled in a steady left-right stroke out to the reef. Forty
miles to the north, the out-islands were sharply silhouetted
against clear blue afternoon sky.

As I was back-paddling to turn myself around for the
homeward trek, I heard a noise coming from a hundred
yards out that sounded like Old Faithful getting ready to

blow. I stared in the direction of the sound and saw plumes of water rise from the sea, followed by unmistakable shapes.

I watched in awe and wonder as a pod of humpback whales leapt and belly-flopped, sending out waves of water that rocked my kayak like a baby's cradle. I laughed at their joyous abandonment and wished Michael were there to share the moment. Seeing the whales reminded me that the start of turtle nesting season was only a month away. And it was exactly one year to the day that I had officially become the general manager of WBZE. Where had the year gone?

I tied onto the reef marker and slipped from my kayak into the tepid saltwater. Clinging to a spare line to avoid being separated from my craft, I lowered myself into the sea until my head was a foot underwater. I held my breath and listened intently.

The whales sang for me. It wasn't the chorus from Beethoven's *Ninth*, or Handel's *Messiah*, but it was the sweetest sound I'd ever heard. I surfaced for another breath and submerged again but the concert was over. I climbed back into Top Banana and continued to watch.

When the pod had sounded, disappearing from view, I reluctantly headed for shore. I was so intent on paddling that it took a few strokes to realize that I was again smelling smoke. Due east a smoke spiral, looking like a waterspout, rose toward the sky.

In less than ten minutes I was back on shore, Top Banana lashed to the top of my car, and heading for home.

Alphonso was waiting in my driveway. "Kelly, I want you to think about evacuating. Pack up what you need and get out. It may not be safe for you to be here tonight. Throw your power breaker before you go and make sure any gas tanks are shut off and disconnected." He got back in his car and turned the key in the ignition, calling out the window, "I'm going to warn your neighbors."

I dragged the kayak behind the house and stashed it in a storage shed, then ran inside to throw some clothes in a duffel. Minx. Where was Minx? I remembered letting her out before I went to work. I couldn't leave without Minx.

I went back outside and began calling Minx as I closed my hurricane shutters to keep the interior of the house free of smoke damage. There was still no sign of Minx when I went back inside to close the sliding shutters on the gallery.

Four o'clock. Minx should be home any minute for dinner. I loaded my car with clothes and cat food, set her wicker carrier next to the car for the trip to the station, then waited for her return.

I was too nervous to sit, so I paced in my small front yard, looking west where the smoke from the first fire had lessened to occasional puffs from a once verdant field now reduced to blackened stubble.

The fire trucks headed east to battle the new fire. My neighbors didn't appear to be taking the fire threat seriously. Perhaps I was overreacting. But the smell of smoke was stronger and the air over my house was no longer clear. A bluish haze hung over the valley separating me from my neighbors.

Five o'clock. Where was that damned cat?

# Chapter
# 12

I LEFT THE house at five-thirty to gauge the progress of the fire. I wasn't going to evacuate if I didn't have to. And not without Minx.

I met the fire trucks heading west. When I pulled over to the side of the road to let the trucks pass, I spotted Alphonso trailing the pack in his police car. He paused alongside me.

"Fire's out, Kelly. You can rest easy tonight."

"Thanks. I feel a lot better. My silly cat hasn't come home yet, and I couldn't leave the house without her."

Alphonso waved and headed back toward town.

I drove home and found Minx sitting outside my kitchen door, tail thumping impatiently. She yowled and thrashed when I tried to pick her up. I went into the kitchen, peeled back the foil lid from a square tin of her favorite Sheba shrimp and salmon, a treat reserved for special occasions, and bent down to empty the contents in her food dish. She shoved my hand aside impatiently with her head, then stuck her face in the bowl. Chomp,

chomp, chomp. "Manners, Minx," I muttered as I went outside to reopen the hurricane shutters.

I had two phone calls that night.

The first came after dinner from Benjamin. We chatted about the brush fires. There was no clue as to their origin. They could have been started by a cigarette carelessly tossed from a car window, or even generated by sunlight through a discarded glass bottle. Neither of us wanted to utter the word "arson" aloud.

"I've got news," said Benjamin. "Miss Maude says the fish she served Saturday night was dolphin. I confirmed it when I found her trash bag at the dump Monday afternoon."

"Taking up bin diving, are we, Benjamin?"

He laughed. "Camille wouldn't even let me in the house until I hosed down outside. She threatened to burn my clothes."

"How did you know it was Miss Maude's trash?"

"That part was easy. Not many people drink vintage champagne with dinner. The empty bottle was a dead giveaway."

"Victoria said dolphin and tuna are safe from ciguatera. So, it wasn't fish poisoning after all. I'm so relieved."

"Looks like we all had a touch of flu," said Benjamin. "There's an epidemic of it in the States this winter. A new strain that comes on suddenly."

"Most tourists come here by plane. Sitting for hours in that recycled air where other passengers have been hacking and wheezing, spraying germs. Yuck. Remind me not to kiss any tourists." I paused and changed the subject. "Benjamin, could you have a word with Chris Edwards? He's been telling everyone he was poisoned by Miss Maude."

"I have a meeting scheduled with Chris tomorrow morning on security for the royal visit. Telling him to zip his lip about Miss Maude is the first item on my agenda."

"How is Miss Maude?"

"She was sick Sunday, but she's fine now. Her phone was out of order for a couple of days, but it was repaired late this afternoon."

"And Miss Lucinda?"

Benjamin chuckled. "You know Miss Lucy. She can't stand being ignored or upstaged. She says she was sicker than anyone at the party, but between us? She polished off the better part of a fifth of Tanqueray that night. I think all she had was a bad case of juniper berry flu."

Getting up at four-fifteen every weekday morning plays hell with my beauty sleep. The second call came at ten-twenty after I'd already turned off my light and was snuggled under the covers. "Come on, machine, pick up," I groused from the depths of my favorite pillow. After the fourth ring and my "Talk now or bite your tongue and go to your room" message, I heard Michael's voice. "Mama, this is important. Pick up."

Damn. I'd forgotten to turn off the phone and douse the volume on the answering machine. I stumbled across the darkened room to my desk. "I'm here, Michael. Talk fast before I wake up."

"Sit down, Mama. You've got a personnel problem. I'm no stool pigeon, but I thought you'd want to know about it."

I sighed. "Couldn't whatever it is wait until morning?" I answered my own question by adding, "Go ahead, tell me now."

"Rick and his filly du jour were going at it on your office couch when I arrived at the station tonight."

"During his air shift? What were they doing?"

"Mama, do I have to draw you a picture? They were both in the buff."

I took a deep breath. "What happened? What did you do?"

"They got dressed faster than firemen at a five-alarm. The chick split. Rick went back in the studio, and I hung out in the music room until his shift was over."

"What was Rick's attitude?"

"He was pretty embarrassed. I didn't think it was my place to say anything to him."

"Thanks, Michael. I'll deal with it tomorrow."

"Sweet dreams, Mama."

I went back to bed, but had a difficult time getting back to sleep. Whatever made me decide to buy a radio station? I must have been out of my mind.

# Chapter
# 13

I PONDERED MICHAEL'S phone call on the twenty-minute drive to WBZE the following morning. It was still dark at five-fifteen—sunrise isn't until almost seven in February although the sky begins to lighten an hour before the sun actually pops over the horizon. I drove with my brights on in case any early-morning joggers were out. Abby said she always ran from five to seven. Where did she get the energy? I can barely pop the top on a Tab can that early in the morning.

It was also Groundhog Day. But who on St. Chris, aside from transplanted Statesiders, knew from groundhogs? The closest we come is the mongoose, imported to kill rats in the cane fields. A major error in judgment. Rats are nocturnal and climb trees; mongeese stick to the ground and sleep at night. I looked through the windshield at the stars dotting the sky and knew that if Pennsylvania's Punxsutawney Phil or Wisconsin's Prince Rupert or any other anthropomorphic woodchuck happened to be residing in St. Chris on this particular Wednesday, a shadow would be seen and six more weeks of winter would ensue. Which was good news for the St. Chris Department of Tourism and the hotel association. I decided next year WBZE would sponsor a Mongoose Festival.

I slurped a Tab while I drove, and when my brain finally kicked in, I realized I had two solutions to my personnel problem. I could ignore Michael's phone call or I could confront Rick when he came to work. I chose the latter course. But then what? Rick was over eighteen and I . . . well, I was old enough to be his mother. But I didn't have any kids and this was no time for me to take up parenting. The extent of my parenting skills was keeping Minx from clawing my couch cushions. It also wasn't my job to monitor anyone's sex life. But, on the other hand, it was *my* radio station, *my* office, *my* couch, Rick was *my* employee, and he'd screwed up on the job. Literally. And big time.

After lunch I went to the hardware store and bought a deadbolt lock set, which I installed that afternoon on my office door. Then I sat down to do paperwork until Rick arrived for work.

Rick had been with the station for four years, a year longer than Michael. He'd begun as part of the WBZE weekend crew his freshman year in high school. Now he was graduating in four months, then going to college in the States to study broadcast journalism. He'd gotten a partial scholarship, based on his good grades and my glowing recommendation. After Gilda, Rick was one I'd counted on while I was still the general manager, prior to Mrs. H's return from her six-month cruise and my buying the station before she split for permanent residence in Italy with her new husband Marcello, to help me keep WBZE on the air while Michael and the part-timers were dealing with storm stress and property damage.

I really hated having to chew Rick's ass. If I fired him,

I was hurting him and myself. I needed the help. I still hadn't hired a receptionist and would also have to hire a replacement for Rick before he went away to school in the fall.

At four o'clock I moved to the receptionist desk and sat playing Free Cell on the computer. I was on a twelve-game winning streak when Rick walked in the front door, schoolbooks tucked under his arm, for his 5 P.M. to 10 P.M. shift. It was part of our deal that he could do his homework while he was on the air. But that deal did not include lab sessions in anatomy.

His face blanched when he saw me. "Uh, Kel . . . I mean Ms. Ryan. I didn't expect to find you here."

I knew then I wasn't going to fire him. "Come to my office, Rick." I motioned toward the couch. "Have a seat."

He sat on the edge of the couch, looking as if he were sitting on hot coals. "I'm really sorry about last night."

I raised my hand before he could say anything more or embarrass us both. "You know the rules. No visitors during working hours. If it happens again, you're fired. Now, get to work. You've got a show to do."

Rick breathed a sigh of relief and reached out to shake my hand. "Thanks, Ms. Ryan. I need this job for college money. I promise you I won't screw up again."

I smiled. "It's still Kelly, Rick."

"You won't tell anyone? My father would kill me."

I shook my head. Rick's father was a fundamentalist minister of the hellfire and damnation school. "This stays between us. I promise you that Michael will also keep his mouth shut."

Rick sighed again and turned to leave my office. I called softly after him. "Rick? Do me a favor?"

Before hearing my request, he looked at me and nodded eagerly.

"Practice safe sex."

He blushed and headed off to the music room.

I picked up my purse, locked my office door, and left the station to meet Michael for a quick dinner at the Lower Deck.

When I arrived at Dockside, Michael's Harley was nowhere to be seen; but Victoria and Chris were sharing a table in a rear corner of the Lower Deck with their heads bent over wineglasses, menus, and notepads.

There are two restaurants at the Dockside Hotel. The Lower Deck and Posh Nosh. The Lower Deck is basically a burger, fish and chips, and barbeque joint with umbrella-covered tables scattered across the brick forecourt overlooking the sea. Food is served in baskets or on paper plates nestled in wicker holders; drinks come in plastic cups. Upstairs at Posh Nosh, elegance rules with linen tablecloths, a printed menu, fresh flowers on every table, and prices that rival my monthly food allowance. Michael and I usually eat at the Lower Deck.

I picked a table for two next to the boardwalk, and sat down to read a paperback mystery while I waited for Michael.

The waitress came to take my drink order. "We have Tuborg and Carlsberg on special tonight."

I groaned. "Not you, too?"

"Excuse me?" she said.

I decided to go easy on her. "I'll have a Tuborg and a glass of ice."

She brought my beer and handed me a printed form listing most of the Isabeya restaurants and bars. The square next to the Lower Deck had been stamped with a tiny red and white Danish flag. "There's a promotion going on this month. If you buy either a Tuborg or Carlsberg at every place on this list and have your form stamped, you're eligible for a drawing for a free case of beer." I thanked her and pocketed the form.

Chris stopped at my table on his way out. "And how are you feeling tonight?"

"Fine, Chris. How are you?"

"Better. Although I don't think I'll ever eat fish again. That was a very poor choice on Maude's part."

"Chris, did you meet with Benjamin this morning?" I asked, barely able to contain my annoyance.

"No, I had to cancel at the last minute. Why?"

"Then perhaps you don't know that it wasn't fish poisoning that made you sick. Miss Maude served dolphin that night, which is perfectly safe. I think you should stop spreading those nasty rumors and apologize to Miss Maude immediately."

"Has this been verified?" asked Chris.

"Yes. Benjamin pulled Miss Maude's trash from the dump."

Chris looked at me for a long moment. "I see," he said finally. "If I've been in error, I'll rectify it. Thanks for letting me know." He left the table and headed down the boardwalk toward Government House.

Michael roared up to the Lower Deck on his Harley in the waning light of the setting sun. The bell at the Anglican church on the far end of Kongens Gade tolled six as Michael chained his bike to a light post.

"What are you drinking, Mama?"

"Tuborg. It's the in thing this month." I fished the promotion flyer out of my pocket. "If we drink our way around Isabeya, we'll be eligible for a drawing for a free case."

"Free beer is free beer." He walked up to the bar and returned with a bottle of Carlsberg Elephant.

Victoria waved from the staircase on her way upstairs to change for hostessing at Posh Nosh. "Pop up and see me before you go home, Kelly."

The waitress appeared with a small plate. "*Smørrebrød.*

Compliments of Miss Victoria." On the plate were a dozen small rounds of bread with various toppings.

I picked up a silver dollar-sized round of rye topped with liver pate garnished with a sliver of chopped egg and a leaf of parsley, and popped it in my mouth. The pate was smoother on my tongue than butter. "Oh, this is good. Michael, try one. The chef at the Watering Hole should take lessons. This beats any of that pseudo-Danish crap he's dishing out at lunch."

After we had emptied the plate, which took all of two minutes, Michael leaned across the table. "Did you talk to Rick?" he asked with a gleam in his eye.

"I did and it's over and done. Wipe that silly smirk off your face. I promised Rick we'd keep our mouths shut. He doesn't want his father to find out."

"If I had Rick's father, I'd either be a eunuch or celibate."

"Bite your tongue." I edged my foot out of my sandal and slid my bare foot up Michael's calf. Michael grinned and reached under the table to grab my foot. "Did you recognize the girl Rick was with?"

"I thought it looked like one of Angie's cousins. But I really didn't get a good look at her face."

I wriggled my foot from Michael's grasp to jab him with my toes before slipping on my sandal.

"Not from the Ramirez side of the family?" I'd had a run-in with the Ramirez twins almost a year ago. It wasn't something I wanted to press in my book of memories. Those boys were bad news bears.

"No, Barbara's side. Could have been one of her daughters." Barbara was Abby's secretary and related to Angie, Pete's new wife.

"Damn. I'm going to forget we had this conversation. The last thing I need is to have Barbara accuse me of running a bawdy house at WBZE."

"Mama—or should I call you madam?—I know it's ancient history for you, but have you forgotten what it was like to be eighteen?" He began humming "Aquarius" under his breath.

I reached over and pinched his arm. Hard. "Shut up, Michael."

"Would you like another round of beer?" I looked up in surprise at the waitress who'd crept up to our table, like Carl Sandburg's "Fog," on her little cat feet. "We have fish and chips tonight."

Michael and I both turned faintly green at the mention of fish. "One Tuborg was enough for me. I feel a bit woozy. I'll have an iced tea and a Swiss cheeseburger, medium-rare." Michael opted for cheddar on his burger and a large Coke. The waitress trotted off to place our orders.

"Michael. I forgot to tell you. Benjamin found out the fish we had at Miss Maude's was dolphin. He says we all had the flu and the fish had nothing to do with it."

"Mama, I'm no Einstein when it comes to math, but it doesn't take a Vegas bookie to figure the odds on nine people all getting sick at the same time." He rubbed his temples with his fingertips. "Do you have any aspirin on you? I've got a headache. That Carlsberg is potent stuff."

Michael felt much better after we had eaten, and he offered to treat me to ice cream at Maubi's "Hot to Trot" roach coach, parked in its usual spot a few yards away on the Isabeya waterfront, before he had to head off to work. I said I'd meet him at Maubi's and ran upstairs to see Victoria. The Posh Nosh bartender said Victoria hadn't come down to hostess for dinner. She was sick as a dog with the flu.

# Chapter
# 14

"ONE SCOOP OR TWO, Morning Lady?" Maubi sat on a backless swivel stool inside his van, holding an ice cream scoop in midair, waiting for my answer. Michael was standing outside the van next to the serving window, bent over a double-dip cone, losing his valiant battle to keep chocolate dribbles from running down his arm.

"Victoria's sick with the flu," I said. "Funny, she looked fine an hour or so ago."

Maubi put the scoop back in the rinse bucket and stood up to reach for a screw-top jar that had formerly held chunky peanut butter—I easily recognized the bright blue plastic lid—from a top shelf inside his van. "Bush. A little bush will fix Miss Victoria up just fine." He pulled a snack-size plastic bag from a box and began shaking some of the contents of the jar into the bag. He ran his fingers across the top of the bag, sealing it shut, then handed it to me. "You take this to Miss Victoria straight away. Tell her two heaping spoons in a cup of boiling water. Steep five minutes, then drink. She do that every couple hours and she be right as rain by morning."

I ran back to Dockside, begged a carafe of hot water and a cup from the Posh Nosh kitchen, then knocked on the door of Victoria's suite. "Vic, it's Kelly. I know you're not feeling well, but please open the door."

Victoria looked worse than I'd felt Sunday morning. She flapped a hand in my direction, suddenly clamped it over her mouth, then ran to the loo, slamming the door. I set the tray on a table and began preparing the bush tea according to Maubi's directions. When Victoria emerged a few minutes later, mopping her face with a damp cloth, the tea was ready. I put the cup in her hand. "Bottoms up, Vic."

"What is it?"

"Bush tea. Maubi sent me with it. He said to drink a cup every two hours and you'll be fine by morning. Two heaping spoonfuls in boiling water. Let the brew steep for five minutes before drinking."

I left Victoria standing with the cup in her hand and quietly closed the door to her suite.

Michael and Maubi were deep in conversation when I got back to the van. Michael's back was to me and I couldn't hear what they were saying.

Maubi spotted me first and quickly picked up his ice cream scoop, saying in a voice slightly louder than normal, "What'll it be, Morning Lady? I got coconut and a little bit of pineapple. Those be two of your favorites."

The combination was pure piña colada in a cup, minus the rum. A blissful moment on the lips, an agonizing lifetime of sit-ups on the hips. But definitely worth it for Maubi's homemade ice cream.

Michael wiped a bit of pineapple from my chin, then kissed me. "Gotta run, Mama. Duty calls. See you in the

A.M." He headed off in the direction of Dockside to fetch his bike. The Anglican church bell rang the half hour. Eight-thirty. Almost my bedtime, but Michael didn't go on the air until ten. I kept my thoughts to myself.

Maubi slipped an extra scoop of coconut into my nearly empty cup. I recognized a diversionary tactic when I saw one and also realized that Maubi wanted to chat. "How is Miss Victoria?" he said.

"I left her with a cup of bush tea in her hand. What's in it?"

Maubi smiled. "Little of this, little of that. Some wild basil, a bit of worryvine. Old recipe of my grandmama's. She be a weed woman."

"Really? That's fascinating. I've heard of the weed women, but I've never known one." The weed women were part of our plantation heritage. Medical doctors were scarce on St. Chris during the sugar days, but each plantation boasted a weed woman who used local herbs and shrubs to cure the sick. The lore of the weed women was passed from generation to generation; but in the days of over-the-counter cure-alls, the St. Chris weed women were slowly becoming extinct.

"You ask Miss Maude. She be one, too. She learn from my grandmama. In the old days they hitch up the cart and go out in the hills every week. Don't go out by yourself, Morning Lady. Plants are like people. Sometimes the most pleasing to the eye be the most deadly." He leaned across the serving counter, putting us at eye level. "The pink plant. My grandmama call it wormgrass. That plant look sweet, sweet with all pretty pink and white flowers. But that plant kill cattle. Even a little bitty bite. Grandmama say in the old, old days, way before the gallows, pink plant used to kill prisoners." He nodded solemnly. "You go to the bush, keep your hands safe in your pocket. You need bush for whatever ails you, you come to Maubi."

A cluster of tourists exited from a taxi van idling near Government House, chattering as they approached "Hot to Trot." I thanked Maubi for the ice cream and turned toward my car. Maubi called after me, "Quincy coming home from college for Ag Fair. He ask me to tell you." Quincy was Maubi's son, studying hotel management in his first year on scholarship at Cornell.

"Tell Quincy I can't wait to see him." I waved to Maubi and headed for home. I thought about Quincy and wondered what he was going to do for a summer job. He'd run the water sports pavilion at Harborview for several years, but the hotel was closed for remodeling. I made a mental note to talk to Victoria. Between us we could probably find Quincy a job.

As I got closer to home, I saw that the east end was again ablaze.

# Chapter
# 15

THE FIRE WAS consuming portions of the north shore on the sea side of the road. I sat on my gallery, Minx at my side, and watched anxiously as the small cove where I moored Top Banana became a ring of fire. But I breathed a deep sigh of relief when I remembered that Top Banana was safely dry-docked in the storage shed behind my house.

The trade winds had died at sunset, but the fire moved slowly westward of its own accord like a grazing beast. Fire trucks lined the side of the road, but the firefighters stood next to the trucks watching the fire consume itself. Water was, as always, in short supply—we depend on rainfall for our drinking water—and not to be wasted.

St. Chris was no stranger to fire. It was fire—one wag had dubbed it Danish lightning—that destroyed Isabeya in early 1764. Isabeya, which prior to the fire consisted of a haphazard conglomeration of buildings erected by the Arawak Indians, the Spanish, English, French, and Knights of Malta, was rebuilt by the Danes in a six-by-six grid pattern that still exists, along with most of the Danish-constructed buildings, today. It was fire that the planters used to clear land for planting sugar cane, and fire that ate the stubble after the cane had been harvested so the fields could be easily replanted.

After Gilda, Miss Maude told me that hurricanes are nature's cleanser. I wondered what she would say about fire.

"Fire," she said the next afternoon while we sat on her front gallery drinking iced tea, "fire is man's destroyer." She topped our glasses from a cut crystal pitcher, the same one that held swizzles on Saturday mornings. "Man uses fire to destroy that which he no longer has any use for. Like the hardwood forests that were burned to clear land for planting cane. But man also uses fire to create." She pointed to the pitcher.

"When I lived in Chicago," I said, caressing the cut crystal with my fingertips, "I spent part of one summer in northern Wisconsin with friends who were glassblowers. They had a summer studio in the woods where they did glassblowing under the stars. The summer tourists used to come and watch, and in the morning we'd find boxes of pastry left on the doorstep in lieu of thank-you notes."

I remembered sitting in a clearing in the pine woods, watching great globs of molten glass, looking like iridescent comets against the inky black sky, transformed in a slowly exhaled breath into vases and bowls of incredible beauty. My hosts had only one room wired for electricity and the sole outhouse was located in a thicket full of wasps, but every time I hear Bob Dylan croon "Lay, Lady, Lay," I'm back in that pine woods watching glassblowing under the stars. One morning a flautist from Boston, summering in Wisconsin, awakened me with a concert under my loft window that sounded as exquisite as a nightingale.

Miss Maude rocked and smiled. "Those must be happy memories for you."

I nodded and changed the subject. "Tell me how you're feeling."

"Perfectly fine. I hope you and Michael have recovered as well."

"Miss Maude," I said, reaching over to place my hand on her arm, "you must go ahead with the royal dinner. We all know it wasn't the fish. I had a little talk with Chris Edwards last night. I hope he got in touch with you."

"Dear Christopher sent a note tucked in a floral arrangement that was delivered this morning," said Miss Maude. "Go inside and look. The flowers are on a table in the living room."

Chris had very expensive taste. Filling a large vase were two-dozen pink and white roses. The last time I stopped at Dahlia's florist shop, roses were sixty dollars a dozen. Like everything else, they were flown in, which added considerably to the cost. At those prices I wasn't expecting roses from Michael on Valentine's Day.

I went back out to the gallery.

"I spoke with Her Majesty earlier today," said Miss Maude. "When she mentioned how much she and Prince Henrik were looking forward to the dinner, I knew I couldn't disappoint her. But I think I'll change the menu and serve a Danish ham for the main course."

"I think that would be appropriate," I said.

"The royal party is coming on the yacht *Dannebrog*," said Miss Maude. "They'll be traveling with the *Danmark*, the training ship for the Danish Merchant Marine. Have you ever seen the *Danmark* under full sail? It's most impressive."

"Only on telly in a tall ships parade, never in person."

Miss Maude went into the living room and returned

with a scrapbook. "Here's a picture taken the last time the *Danmark* was here on St. Chris." I looked at a photo of the three-masted *Danmark* under full sail, with the red and white Danish pennant flying from the stern. "The *Danmark* was built of steel in 1933. After serving briefly for the Allies, it went to Connecticut, where it was used as a training ship for American cadets until the end of World War II. I know the captain rather well, so I've invited him to dine with us. I'm certain he'll be glad to give you a tour of the ship."

"I would enjoy that. Thank you."

"Am I included in that invitation?" Benjamin inquired as he approached the front gallery from the kitchen side of Miss Maude's house.

"Benjamin, you gave me a fright!"

"I meant to," he replied with a smile.

"Have you been demoted to foot patrol?" I asked.

"I'm doing a perimeter check. Miss Maude, you've got a security problem."

"Don't start with me, Benjamin."

"Miss Maude, you need to face reality. This isn't Christmas morning. You can't repel potential assassins with coconuts swinging on ropes."

Miss Maude allowed herself a small smile and offered Benjamin a glass of iced tea. "What do you suggest?"

"A perimeter fence. Preferably topped with razor wire."

"Papa did not believe in fences."

"Your father lived in a different time when people respected property rights." Having made his point, Benjamin sat back in his chair.

Miss Maude sighed. "I loathe the very idea of a fence."

"It doesn't have to be permanent. You can have it removed as soon as the royal visit is over."

"Perhaps."

"The alternative is to move the dinner to a secure location. Miss Maude, I simply don't have enough men for a cordon around your house."

"You win, Benjamin. But I draw the line at razor wire."

Benjamin smiled. "A fence will be adequate. Island Lumber will be here in the morning to take measurements."

"What about a wood fence?" I said. "The school children could decorate it with murals of St. Chris."

Miss Maude beamed. "What an excellent idea. The Queen is an accomplished artist; she will be charmed. I'll phone Amelia now to arrange for the art students." Miss Maude hurried into the house, calling over her shoulder, "Benjamin, how soon can you get the fence erected?"

"Nice going, Kelly. I wish I'd thought of that," said Benjamin, high-fiving me.

Miss Maude returned a few minutes later with a book in her hand. "Amelia is going to talk to the students after school. I thought you might like to see this." She handed me a copy of Tolkien's *Lord of the Rings*. "Queen Margrethe did all the illustrations."

I turned the pages slowly, marveling at the artistic talent that captured the essence of the Tolkien fantasy, then passed the book to Benjamin.

He glanced at the book and put it on the table. "Miss Maude, I hate to bring this up, but I need your help. About last Saturday's dinner . . ."

Miss Maude held up her hand. "I've already decided to serve Danish ham instead of fish."

"I'm not concerned about the food," said Benjamin. "We sent every scrap from your trash to the lab in San Juan and the test results were all negative. I'm wondering what became of the champagne cork."

We turned to stare at Benjamin.

"I found the bottle, the foil, the wire . . ."

"The proper term is cage," Miss Maude corrected gently.

"What is?" said Benjamin.

"The name for the wire securing a champagne cork."

"I always call it the wire thing," I said.

"As I was saying." Benjamin cleared his throat to get our attention. "I found everything but the cork. Do you know where it is?"

"I have no idea."

"Why did you rinse and wipe the champagne bottle before you put it in the trash?"

"I did no such thing, Benjamin. I would have rinsed it out to keep the sugar ants away, but the bottle had already been disposed of when I went to tidy the kitchen. I never gave it another thought."

I hated to tear myself away from this fascinating conversation, but it would soon be rush hour. Isabeya's narrow one-way streets turned into instant gridlock at 5 P.M. and my car had a tendency to overheat in slow-moving traffic.

"Thanks for the iced tea, Miss Maude. I've got to go. I promised to look in on Victoria on my way home. She's got the flu. I want to find out if Maubi's cure worked."

"When did this happen?" asked Benjamin.

"Last night. What are you? The public health nurse? Give it a rest, Benjamin."

"What did Maubi give her?" asked Miss Maude.

"Bush tea. He said it had a little of this, a little of that, but mostly wild basil and worryvine. He also mentioned something else . . . what was it?" I thought for a minute. "Pink plant. That's what he said."

"Lord have mercy! Has that man lost his senses?" exclaimed Miss Maude. "Pink plant is highly poisonous. It acts like strychnine."

"Strychnine. Strychnine." I was thinking out loud.

"Agatha Christie used that once in a book. No, that was cyanide. She was also terribly fond of arsenic."

Benjamin and Miss Maude looked at me as if I'd slipped my trolley. I returned to the subject at hand. "I know Maubi didn't put any pink plant in the bush tea. He was warning me about it. He said you would know."

"I certainly do," said Miss Maude, rising from her chair. "You wait right here." She went into the house and returned with another book. "You remember my father trained as a botanist in Denmark before coming to St. Chris. This is what pink plant looks like." She pointed to a delicate watercolor tipped into the leather-bound volume.

I looked at a small plant that reminded me of a loosely constructed bird's nest, or a very skinny octopus pitching a fit, with thin spikes shooting out from the center like a spider plant. The leaves were grouped in whorls of four, with bell-shaped soft pink flowers gracing the ends of the spikes.

"It's beautiful," I said. "It looks like it should be grown in a hanging basket."

"Kelly, pink plant is nothing for you or anyone else to mess with," Miss Maude said sternly. "Strychnine causes convulsions and almost instant death. If you want to learn about bush remedies, we'll go into the hills together like I used to do with Maubi's grandmother Alveena. Promise me you won't go by yourself. There are deadly poisons growing wild everywhere on this island."

I promised, then picked up my bag. "I've got to go. I want to beat the traffic."

"I'll go with you," said Benjamin. "I need a lift to my car."

We left Miss Maude slowly rocking on her gallery, reading *Lord of the Rings*.

# Chapter
# 16

VICTORIA WAS SNUGLY tucked in her not-so-wee-little bed when Benjamin and I arrived at Dockside. Benjamin waited at the Lower Deck while I trotted up to Victoria's suite. She hung on to the doorjamb, like a limpet clinging to a rock, while we talked.

"Vic, I hope I didn't disturb you."

"Not at all. I had to get up to open the door."

"How are you feeling?"

"Kelly, I'm not up to receiving visitors. Right now all I want to do is go back to bed."

"Didn't the bush tea help at all?"

Victoria smiled wanly. "You were sweet to bring it to me, and please thank Maubi for his thoughtfulness, but strictly between us? I couldn't drink it. Beecham's Powders were the only thing I could keep down. That's my standard cure-all. A friend sends them to me from Boots in London." Vic looked like she was about to crumple. "I hate to be rude, but I really must go back to bed. I'll call you when I'm finally up and about."

I blew a kiss in Victoria's direction and headed down the stairs to the Lower Deck.

Benjamin sat nursing a club soda with lime. The five o'clock traffic was jamming the streets, so I joined him at the table.

"Still on duty?" I asked. "I thought you'd be tossing down a greenie."

"I tried one Tuesday night and it didn't sit well on my stomach."

"Heineken stock must be dropping like a stone. You know, Michael and I had the same thing happen Wednesday night. He had a headache after one Carlsberg, and I felt woozy before I'd finished my Tuborg. We both felt better after we ate."

"Why did you have to mention food?" said Benjamin.

I glanced at Benjamin's Winnie-the-Pooh tummy and wisely said nothing.

"Don't start. Camille is always bringing home no-fat, low-fat, no-taste stuff. She wants me to have only salads for lunch. What's the point of eating if you can't enjoy it?" He called to the waitress for a basket of plantain chips and mango salsa, shooting me a look that said, "Don't tell Camille."

I quickly changed the subject. "What was the big deal with Miss Maude about the missing cork?"

Benjamin was too busy eating to respond immediately. I watched as the last sunbathers caught the ferry from Harborview to Dockside. It was strange to see Harborview dark night after night, the way it had appeared to the Arawak Indians, the pre-Columbian inhabitants of Isabeya who used Papaya Quay for a lookout post. How dumbstruck they must have been on that November day in 1493 when Columbus and his crew appeared in sailing ships bigger than anything they'd ever seen. In two weeks the *Danmark* would sail into the Isabeya harbor, accompanying royal yacht *Dannebrog*, and it would be the biggest sailing ship I'd ever seen. The thought that Columbus had set foot where I now sat, and Queen Margrethe would walk in his footsteps, sent a small shiver running down my spine.

Benjamin pushed aside the empty basket. "That will keep me until dinner. What were you saying?"

"The wine cork."

Benjamin smiled, the age-old smile of a sphinx contemplating the riddle of the ages. "It's like the dog that didn't bark. Think about it." He brushed stray chip crumbs from the front of his navy blue police uniform, then drained the last of the club soda from his glass. "Don't forget we're working on the homestead house Saturday morning. Be there at nine if you can."

I thought about that blasted cork all the way home.

# Chapter
# 17

FRIDAY MORNING I aired *The Beggar's Opera* on the morning classics after the daily Danish lesson. We'd progressed from "Hello, how are you?" to more practical matters like "Where is the bathroom?" and "May I use your telephone?" I knew the Queen would be impressed when those phrases were introduced into the garden party conversation.

While my listeners were regaled by Macheath (James Morris), Lucy Lockit (Joan Sutherland), and Polly Peachum (Kiri Te Kanawa) in a two-hour recording of John Gay's 1728 social satire of politics and music, I retired to the WBZE music room to catch up on filing. After I'd racked more rock albums than I would ever listen to in this or any other lifetime—and posted a sign on the music room wall that read YOU PULL IT, YOU PUT IT BACK—I made out weekly paychecks. I was overjoyed to see that WBZE still had money in the bank, which meant I could afford to hire a receptionist. As soon as the royal visit was over.

After *The Beggar's Opera* I segued into the 1928
*Threepenny Opera*, wherein John Gay's Macheath became Bertolt Brecht and Kurt Weill's Mack the Knife,
and closed the segment by airing Bobby Darin's 1959
double Grammy whammy "Mack the Knife." I ended the
morning with Chuck Mangione's Grammy-nominated album *An Evening of Magic—Chuck Mangione—Live at the
Hollywood Bowl* from his sold-out July 16, 1978, concert.
It was one of those "You had to be there" nights. A live
recording captures the moment, but loses the energy zing-
ing like a palpable force between performer and audience.
Listening to that album reminded me how much I missed
being on stage. I closed my show with Esther Satterfield's
definitive vocal of Mangione's "Land of Make Believe"
recorded live in Toronto in 1973, and left the station humming "Feels So Good" all the way to the Watering Hole.

The gang was already seated and having drinks when
I plopped next to Margo.

"Kel, wait until you hear what's happened," said
Margo.

"Hang on, sweetie. I want to check the specials first,
I'm hungry."

I turned to look at the chalkboard, but it was not in its
usual spot.

"What? The chef ran out of ideas for Danish fare?"

Margo grabbed my face between her hands and turned
it toward her own. "Read my lips, Kel. The chef is gone.
Carole's cooking today. There's only soup and doctor-
them-yourself burgers."

I pried Margo's hands from my cheeks so I could ask,
"What happened to the chef?"

"Split. Took a hike. Gone bush. Who knows?" said
Jerry, reaching for his white-on-white on the rocks.

"He was deported," said Abby, stirring her iced coffee.

"You're kidding!" We sounded like a Greek chorus.

"I saw the whole thing from my office window. Immigration swooped in this morning and nabbed him. I hear his green card had expired."

"It's probably because of the royal visit," said Jerry. "Government House is in a total flap. They can't afford to have anything go wrong. Every time I see Chris, he's either on the phone or tearing off someplace."

Carole called out from the bar. "Burgers are on the grill, guys. Get 'em while they're hot."

After we'd polished off our burgers, Margo pulled a buff envelope from her purse. "Check this, Kel." Inside was an engraved invitation to the Royal Reception and Garden Party.

"I got one, too," said Jerry.

"Mine was in the morning mail," said Abby.

"I haven't been to the post office yet," I said. "I'll head over there after lunch."

"You need your invitation to get in," said Jerry. "They'll also be checking names at the door. Security is really going to be tight."

The rest of the lunch chatter centered around what everyone was going to wear. Jackets and ties, preferably three-piece suits, were a must for the men. Jerry complained loudly about the lack of air-conditioning at Government House.

"Jerry, it's two hours out of your life. Suffer in silence," said Margo. "Heidi will have your head on a platter if you make a fuss. Would you rather be wearing pantyhose and high-heeled shoes?"

Jerry made a face and split for Government House.

Margo continued, "Do we have to wear hats? I hear the Queen loves hats. I wonder if she'll be wearing her crown. I wish I had a tiara."

"I wish I had a new dress," I said. "If only I had time to fly over to San Juan to shop. Everything I have in my closet is either island casual shorts and T-shirts or long skirts and tops."

"I'm going to wear a suit," said Abby. "But no hat. I don't like hats." She fingered the flawless two-carat diamond studs in her ears.

"I'm wearing a dress. And a hat. One with a wide brim. Like they wear at Ascot," said Margo. "Kel, I'll come over to your house tomorrow and we'll root through your closet. You probably have something in there you forgot about."

"I can't tomorrow. I promised Benjamin I'd work on the homestead house."

"No big t'ing. We'll do it Sunday afternoon. You supply the Bloody Marys."

I stopped at the post office before going to check on Victoria. My mailbox was empty, except for a fourth-class flyer advertising a sale that had ended two weeks earlier. I tossed the flyer in the trash basket and headed for Dockside.

Victoria was up and about and attending to paperwork in her office. She popped a wintergreen Tic Tac in her mouth as I entered the room.

"How are you feeling, Vic?"

"Much better, thank you. But now I have a new headache. Three of my staff disappeared this morning. I'm short two maids and a busboy. Why now? The hotel is full and I need every hand I can get." She slid her tongue over her teeth and reached for another mint.

"What happened?"

"Immigration. I hear the Watering Hole chef was deported."

"It's true. I just came from having lunch there. Carole was cooking."

"Now I have to go through every personnel file to make sure the rest of my staff is on the up and up. I can't afford to lose anyone else." She reached for another folder. "Was there something special you wanted?"

"I came to see how you were."

Victoria flashed me a smile. "You're a love. This royal visit is driving me bonkers. Between the luncheon and the garden party, I don't have time to breathe for the next two weeks. Having the flu really set me back. I wish Chris would make up his mind about the wine for the royal lunch. If I don't place an order by Monday, it won't get here in time."

"What's the problem?"

"Chris hasn't decided between red or white. He wants to consult with Denmark first to find out the Queen's preference. I suggested we serve both. We sampled several lovely wines the other evening that would be perfectly adequate, but he said no, we can't have both red and white. It's not in the budget." Another mint went into her mouth.

"Vic, I hate to pry, but what's with the mints? I know you don't smoke, but you look like someone who's trying to kick the habit."

"I can't get the taste of garlic out of my mouth. For the past two days all I can taste is garlic and I don't even like it. Except in a Caesar salad."

"Michael complained of the same thing. Must be a lingering flu symptom. I didn't notice it myself, but I take garlic pills every day with my vitamins."

Victoria looked frazzled and distracted, so I departed. On my way out of her office I saw a familiar buff envelope sitting on top of a stack of unopened mail. Was I the only one who hadn't received my invitation to the royal garden party?

# Chapter
## 18

UNDER A BRIGHT cloudless sky with a temperature pushing ninety but feeling cooler because of the trade winds, the fairground was bustling with Ag Fair preparations.

While the homestead house building crew hammered away, the food and souvenir vendors were busy repainting their wooden booths, farmers were cleaning out livestock pens, and the ground crew was mowing the field where the midway rides would be set up. Inside the main exhibit hall, the freshly swept floor was being striped with masking tape to mark off the floor space devoted to school exhibits, plant sellers, and down-island purveyors of produce, jams, spices, and hot sauce.

Maubi's "Hot to Trot" van was parked near the building site and doing a brisk business in cold drinks, fried chicken legs, and beef, chicken or saltfish pates.

"Trevor! Are you working or eating?" Benjamin called out to his son after Trevor's fifth trip to the van. "We need more nails."

"I'm doing both." Trevor's voice was heard through the

van's service window. He climbed onto Maubi's backless stool and stuck his head out the window. "I'm helping Maubi in the van while he works on the house."

"Nails, Trevor. Now!"

Trevor hopped out of the van to fetch a box of nails.

By midday the floor of our fifteen-by-thirty-foot structure was in place. Because we were building a replica, not a habitable dwelling, we omitted the cistern—saving ourselves hours of backbreaking digging in the blazing tropic sun—but for authenticity had cut a cistern hatch cover in the living room floor.

Our next step was framing the dwelling. Building the homestead house reminded me of an exquisitely made Japanese doll house—complete with shoji screens, parquet floors, a tiled roof, and a tiny vase of flowers placed on a low table—I had played with as a child. The house came apart like a puzzle. If you knew in which order to remove the pieces.

Benjamin called a lunch break. As everyone clustered around Maubi's van, Trevor ran over to me clutching a pate—a favorite Caribbean snack resembling a turnover or a Cornish pastie, consisting of a spicy chopped filling encased in pastry that is either baked or fried—in each hand. "Which one do you want, Miss Kelly? Beef or chicken?" He held out his hands, then paused, a puzzled look crossing his face. "I forgot which is one is chicken."

"I like both, Trevor. You pick first and I'll take the other one."

"We could take a small bite out of each one, then we'd know for true." He bit into the pate in his left hand. "This is beef."

I reached for the uneaten pate in his right hand. "I'll take this one. I really like chicken." I took a big bite and almost gagged when the spicy filling connected with my taste buds. "This one's saltfish." I never order saltfish, although Maubi asks every time I buy a pate at "Hot to Trot."

"I like saltfish," said Trevor. "Can I have that one?"

I gladly swapped and reached for a bottle of water to wash away the lingering taste of saltfish before diving into the chicken pate.

"Are you through?" Trevor asked before I swallowed the last mouthful. "Let's go explore the sugar factory." He tugged at my hand. "My class came here on a field trip. I know all about it. I'll show you."

We headed across the newly mowed field, cross-cut to a blunt-topped stubble that looked like beige Astro turf but would easily slash bare feet to ribbons, to the complex that was once called Central Factory and was now a museum commemorating the Golden Days of Sugar.

"See these tracks?" Trevor pointed to the ground where parallel ruts were periodically joined by wooden ties. "That's where the railroad ran."

"A railroad? Here on St. Chris?"

"It was a small one, like they have at Disney World. Did you ever go on the Big Thunder Mountain Railroad in the Magic Kingdom? I went four times."

I didn't have the heart to tell Trevor that one of the worst experiences of my adult life was riding the little train from hell in Frontierland. I also hated crack-the-whip when I was a kid. Ferris wheels and roller coasters? The very thought of them makes me queasy. I have this thing about heights.

"After the cane was cut in the fields, it was loaded in bundles on little flatcars at the sugar plantations and brought here to Central Factory."

"What happened to the railroad?" I asked.

"My teacher said it got sold. She thinks it's in Mexico. Do they grow sugar cane in Mexico?"

"I don't know, Trevor. You could ask your mom, or look it up at the library."

We'd reached the main two-story building.

"The cane cars stopped there." Trevor pointed to a small shed. "Let's go inside and I'll show you the rest."

The Central Factory doors were locked so we continued our tour by peering through dusty windows.

"First the cane was ground in the crusher to get out all the juice. Then the juice was boiled in big basins called clarifiers and then in little basins called coppers. My mom has an old copper in our front yard. She plants flowers in it."

"How did the juice become sugar?" I asked.

"I forget. If we could get inside, I'd remember. But I know the factory was built here because of the stream flowing through the gut. They needed the water."

"You can take me inside during the Ag Fair," I said. "I think I'd better get back to work on the homestead house. But first, let's get some ice cream from Maubi. My treat."

Trevor and I ran back across the field to Maubi's van.

By late afternoon the homestead house was completely framed. The building crew sat on the narrow front gallery, swinging our legs to ease our aching muscles, swigging cold Heineken. It tasted great.

Benjamin walked around the outside of the house, ending back at the gallery. "If we get an early start tomorrow, we should be finished by late afternoon. Next weekend we'll paint the outside gray to look like stone, and put up the outhouse. Camille and Amelia have been collecting furniture and old utensils to put in the kitchen. Miss Maude donated a bolt of fabric to make the divider in the bedroom and curtains for the windows. We'll furnish the house right before the fair opens."

Michael and I were supposed to go to dinner at Jerry's

house that Saturday night. But Michael was still feeling rocky from the flu. By the time I got home it was almost six, and I was too pooped from toiling all day in the hot sun to go anywhere but to bed.

# Chapter
## 19

I TRIED CALLING Margo at home early Sunday morning to hear about dinner at Jerry's and beg off rummaging through my closet, but all I got was her answering machine. I left a message on the machine, and another tacked to my kitchen door, then headed for the fairground.

The homestead house was looking damned good. We were the only group working at the fairground that morning—everyone else was in church, at home after a late Saturday night, or heading for the beach. When we took a break at ten-thirty, we'd finished putting up the exterior plywood and had the outside window shutters, front and back doors, corrugated tin roof, and outhouse to go before we were through for the day.

We were all sitting on the homestead house gallery chugging cool water when Benjamin's beeper sounded. He checked the message, then ran to his Blazer for his cell phone. After a brief conversation, he yelled to me from the parking lot. "Kelly, grab your gear and get over here."

I picked up my water jug and fanny pack, and trotted over to Benjamin's vehicle.

"Get in. That was Miss Maude calling from Miss Lucy's house. Something is seriously wrong."

We headed for the south shore, a few miles west of Leatherback Bay where the sea turtles nested, arriving at the pillars marking the entrance to Miss Lucinda's property in a dead heat with an ambulance approaching from the opposite direction. Benjamin slowed to let the ambulance enter first, then followed closely behind.

The narrow dirt road, bordered on both sides with royal palms debilitated by Gilda but showing signs of recovery, suddenly gave way to a circular driveway. Benjamin pulled in front of the two-story stone house and parked next to Miss Maude's Land Rover. When I got a good look at the house, my mouth dropped open to my knees.

Miss Lucinda lived in a magnificent great house, built in the early 1800s during the glory days of sugar. A ballast brick welcoming arms staircase led to a pair of wrought iron gates in front of the formal second-floor entrance. Miss Maude, dressed in her Sunday going-to-church best accessorized with spotless white gloves and a matching straw hat, waited for us at the top of the stairs. She opened the gates as paramedics dashed up the stairs with a gurney.

A third car sped into the circular driveway. Dr. Williams, the elderly GP who served as the island medical examiner, ran the St. Chris Hospital, and endeared himself to all his female patients by addressing them as "young lady" regardless of age, got out of his car and headed for the stairs, taking them two at a time. Benjamin and I followed, one step at a time, on his heels.

"I found Lucy in the library," said Miss Maude.

I wiped my work-grimed hands on the back of my

shorts, then took her trembling hands in mine. We walked into the house.

The high-ceiling rooms were tastefully furnished with handwoven Persian carpets glowing like a ransom of jewels in the late-morning sunlight, and mahogany furniture upholstered in silk. On the white plastered walls were enough framed paintings to fill a gallery at the Met. I peeked in the dining room and saw a crystal chandelier filled with pristine ivory candles suspended from the tray ceiling. "That's the original Lalique fixture," said Miss Maude. "There's a winch in the crawlspace overhead that raises and lowers it."

Miss Lucinda lay on her side on the library's parquet floor. Next to her face was a small pool of vomit.

The paramedics stood by as Dr. Williams knelt to make his examination. He sighed, shook his head, then gently closed Miss Lucinda's eyelids. He rose to his feet, and put his hands on Miss Maude's shoulders.

"Maude, I'm sorry. She's gone."

Miss Maude closed her eyes and nodded. Dr. Williams slid his arms around Miss Maude and held her as the tears fell slowly down her face.

Benjamin and I stood by, rendered helpless by our shock and grief.

Over Miss Maude's shoulder, Dr. Williams mouthed the words "natural causes, get a body bag" to the paramedics and motioned them out of the library. Then he turned to Benjamin. "I think Lucy kept her brandy in that cabinet over there. Bring a bottle and four glasses to the sitting room." He spoke quietly to Miss Maude. "Come, Maude. Let us retire to the sitting room. I think a restorative is in order." With his arm around Miss Maude's shoulders, he led her out of the library and down the hallway.

Benjamin walked over to the cabinet, opened the leaded

glass doors, and gazed at the array of crystal decanters. He lifted the stopper from one and sniffed the contents. He nodded and picked up four small glasses together with the decanter and left the room.

I stayed in the library, waiting for the paramedics to return, and paid silent homage to Miss Lucinda. A line I thought I remembered from *The Great Gatsby*—about showing friendship for a person when they are alive and not after they are dead—flitted through my head and I wished I'd known Miss Lucinda better. I'd always thought of her as a somewhat silly woman, like Aunt Pittypat Hamilton from *Gone With the Wind*. But Miss Lucinda was Miss Maude's closest and oldest friend, and Miss Maude was not known for suffering fools. To my regret, I had obviously erred in my superficial judgment of Miss Lucinda.

I noticed an open bottle of Tanqueray sitting on a side table along with a squat crystal glass edged in cerise, Miss Lucinda's favorite color, lipstick. On the table was a small silver tray bearing a bowl filled with what looked like brightly colored hard-shell Easter candies, the ones usually filled with marshmallow cream. Definitely pushing the season. The market was still trying to pawn off leftover Christmas candy on half-price special. I knew Miss Lucinda had a sweet tooth, but candy mixed with gin? That was a combination guaranteed to make anyone ill.

The library shutters were open to admit fresh air, but the smell of vomit was becoming overpowering. I also smelled gin and a hint of something else. I covered my nose and mouth with my hand, and gazed once again at Miss Lucinda. Her left arm was extended palm down, the diamonds in her wedding rings winking in the sunlight.

The paramedics came back into the room with a black body bag. "You can go now. We'll take over from here."

I left the library and followed the voices to the sitting

room. As I entered the room, I heard Dr. Williams say, "I warned Miss Lucy time and time again that she had to quit drinking. She had ulcers and her liver was in very bad shape. Maude, we both know Lucy was failing and it was only a matter of time. I'm sorry she went this way."

"Excuse me, Dr. Williams, but I don't think it was the gin that killed her," I said. "I think she had the flu."

"What leads you to that diagnosis, young lady?"

"There was the smell of . . ." I ran out of the sitting room back to the library. The body bag was open and the paramedics were getting ready to lift Miss Lucinda from the floor. "Wait! Don't touch her."

Benjamin was right beside me. "What's wrong, Kelly?"

I pointed at Miss Lucinda's bare left wrist.

# Chapter
## 20

BENJAMIN SENT THE paramedics outside, then phoned for police backup and a camera. "I want everything in this room photographed. From every possible angle." He turned to me. "God dammit, Kelly. Why didn't you say something sooner?"

"Don't yell at me, Benjamin. It's like you said the other afternoon at Dockside about the dog that didn't bark. Remember? I didn't realize at first what I was seeing."

"You're right. I'm sorry." He looked around the room. "Why don't you go sit with Miss Maude. I'll stay here."

I headed for the hallway but was stopped by Benjamin's voice. In a kinder, gentler tone he asked, "Kelly, did you notice anything else?"

"The gin bottle and glass on the end table."

"Anything else?"

I shook my head.

Dr. Williams stopped me outside the sitting room. "What made you think Miss Lucy had the flu?"

"I smelled garlic."

"What?"

"Garlic. We all had the flu last week. Me, Michael, Benjamin and Camille, Amelia and Freddy. Miss Maude. And Victoria at Dockside. But Vic wasn't sick at the same time the rest of us were. Michael complained about it first. He said he couldn't get the taste of garlic out of his mouth. Then Vic said the same thing when I talked to her Friday afternoon. I hadn't noticed it myself, but I take garlic pills every day."

Dr. Williams reached into the pocket of his rumpled beige linen jacket for a small notebook, jotted a few words, then went into the library to confer with Benjamin.

I went into the sitting room. Miss Maude was sitting on the edge of a chintz-covered chair, staring into space.

"Miss Maude," I said softly. "Would you like me to take you home?"

"I think I'd like a bit more of that brandy first."

I took the small, stemmed glass from Miss Maude's gloved hand, filled it two-thirds with brandy and gave it back to her, then poured some for myself. We raised our glasses.

"To Miss Lucinda," I said.

Miss Maude nodded and we drank.

"I came to pick up Lucy for church. We always went to the eleven o'clock service at the Anglican church. After church, we'd have Sunday lunch. Then I'd bring Lucy home in time for her nap."

"Where is Miss Lucinda's housekeeper?"

"Elodia always has Saturday afternoon to Sunday afternoon off. She spends the night with her married daughter on the west end. Oh, my. I should telephone her. There's so much to be done. I think I'd like to go home now."

I went back to the library door. "Benjamin?"

He broke off his conversation with Dr. Williams.

"Miss Maude wants to go home. I'll drive her."

"Thank you."

"My car's at the fairground."

"I'll get you back there. Will you stay with Miss Maude until I'm through here?"

I nodded and left the room. Miss Maude and I were approaching the pillars on the south shore road when the backup police unit passed us, heading full speed for the house.

We arrived at Miss Maude's home to find Camille, Trevor, Amelia and her girls, all in church clothes, coming down the steps from Miss Maude's front gallery.

"Granny Maude," said Amelia, "I didn't see you in church this morning. Is everything all right?"

I jumped out of Miss Maude's Land Rover, motioned to Amelia, then whispered in her ear.

"Oh my God. Poor Granny Maude." Amelia quickly recovered her composure and said to Camille, "Take the kids over to your house, will you? Granny Maude's not feeling well. I'll be over in a little bit." She reached in her purse and handed Camille some folded bills. "Stop at McDonald's and get lunch for the kids. Okay?"

"Can Miss Kelly come have lunch with us?" asked Trevor.

"Not today, Trevor," I said. "Another time."

Camille herded the children into her car and took off.

Amelia and I walked with Miss Maude into her house. Miss Maude headed for her bedroom to change out of her church clothes. "I won't be but a minute. Amelia, would you put the kettle on for tea? That little bit of brandy has gone to my head. Kelly, you'll find a fresh tin of Danish biscuits in the pantry."

We went into the kitchen as instructed. While Amelia filled the kettle, she said, "Kelly, what on earth happened?"

"I think Miss Lucinda came down with the flu and choked to death on her own vomit. Miss Maude found her in the library when she went to pick her up for church this morning."

"How awful. Poor Miss Lucy. Poor Granny Maude." She put the kettle on to boil, then looked at my dirt-stained shorts and tank top. "How did you happen to be there?"

"I was working on the homestead house. Miss Maude called Benjamin at the fairground. He asked me to ride along."

Miss Maude quietly entered the kitchen. "It's a good thing Kelly was there. She spotted something everyone else missed. Including myself."

"What was that, Granny Maude?"

"Lucy was not wearing her watch."

"But she never takes it off."

"Come," said Miss Maude. "Let us take the tea tray outside and discuss this matter further. Something has occurred to me."

We settled ourselves on the back gallery with cups of fragrant Earl Grey tea and Danish sugar cookies. Camille's voice floated out to us from the front of the house. "Where is everybody?"

"Out back, Camille."

"I got a neighbor to watch the kids. Tell me what happened."

"Lucy is dead," said Miss Maude, heading to the kitchen for an extra teacup.

"Oh, no." Camille sank into a cushioned wicker chair. "What happened?"

"Wait until Granny Maude comes back," said Amelia, reaching for another cookie. She turned to Camille. "We never had lunch today."

"I brought a bucket of chicken," Camille replied. "It's in the car. I'll go get it."

While we ate fried chicken and licked our fingers clean, Miss Maude and I related the events of the morning to Amelia and Camille.

"Aside from the missing watch," said Miss Maude, "it occurred to me while I was changing out of my church clothes that Lucy must have had a visitor before she died."

"What makes you say that?" asked Amelia.

"Because she was found in the library."

We all looked at Miss Maude, but said nothing.

"You had to know Lucy's habits. Lucy was very much a creature of habit and each room in her house had a special purpose. For example, meals were always served in the dining room." Miss Maude watched us helping ourselves to Danish cookies from the tin and smiled. "Lucy never ate so much as a cracker that was not served properly on a china plate with a linen napkin beside it. She had no use for the conveniences of paper plates and paper napkins. To her anything made of plastic was an abomination."

"You were saying about the library?" I asked.

"Bear with me, Kelly, I'm trying to collect my thoughts." Miss Maude sipped her tea, then continued. "Lucy used two rooms for her informal entertaining. Her beloved sitting room where she tended to her daily correspondence, and the library. The sitting room was for close female friends and the library was for men. Strangers and couples were received in the formal living room."

"What's the point, Granny Maude?"

Miss Maude looked at me and winked. "Why don't you tell us, Kelly."

"Before Miss Lucinda died, she entertained a male visitor. Someone she knew."

"Very good, Kelly. You may go to the head of the class."

Amelia and Camille laughed. "Kelly, coming from Granny Maude, that's high praise."

"Wait a minute," I said. "I just thought of something else."

Miss Maude looked at me inquiringly.

"Whoever it was brought her a bottle of gin."

"How do you know that?"

"Because it hadn't been decanted. The rest of the ordinary liquor—scotch, brandy, vodka, gin—were all in crystal decanters in the glass-fronted library cupboard. Only the exotic liquors, like Tia Maria or Benedictine, were still in the original bottles lined up behind the decanters." I looked around the table. "Now I've got a question for everyone. Last week, when we all had the flu, did you notice anything unusual?"

"Like what, Kelly?" asked Camille. "I was too sick to pay attention to anything."

"Me, too," said Amelia. "All I wanted to do was curl up and die." She clamped her hand over her mouth. "Granny Maude, I'm so sorry. I didn't mean that literally."

Miss Maude reached over to hug her granddaughter. "It's all right, Amelia. Lucy was my friend for over sixty years and I will miss her every day of my life. But life does go on." Miss Maude clapped her hands together. "What we all need right now is a swizzle. I know Lucy would approve." She picked up the tea tray and chicken bucket and headed for the kitchen.

When we had raised our glasses to Miss Lucinda, Camille asked, "Why did you want to know about the flu, Kelly?"

"I wondered if you'd noticed anything unusual?"

"Like what?"

"Like a funny taste that lasted for a day or so afterward."

Camille licked her lips and thought for a minute. "You know, I did. Garlic. I kept tasting garlic."

"Freddy said that, too. I felt like I'd been chewing on aluminum foil. A metallic sort of aftertaste."

"Lucy's ulcer wouldn't tolerate garlic. So I seldom used it," said Miss Maude. "There was no garlic in anything I prepared for dinner that evening."

# Chapter
## 21

CAMILLE DROPPED ME off at the fairground late Sunday afternoon. The building crew had already left and mine was the only car remaining in the parking lot. The gates to the fairground were locked, but I could see that the homestead house had acquired its roof and shutters. There were still gaping holes where doors needed to be hung, but we had one more weekend to complete the project.

Although I had the road to myself, no cars ahead or behind me, I drove slowly down Kongens Gade paying strict observance to the twenty-mile-an-hour Isabeya speed limit. I'd had one swizzle too many—more than one was one too many in my book—and I didn't need a DUI to add to the headache I was sure to have Monday morning.

The bell in the Anglican church tolled six. The sky was quickly fading to that brief interlude between day and dark we call twilight. Streetlights winked on and illuminated the strings of tiny red and white Danish flags that crisscrossed the street like a cat's cradle to welcome

Queen Margrethe and Prince Henrik. I noticed that the Danish signs on the street corners had been refurbished in anticipation of the royal visit.

Even Government House was silent and dark, devoid of its workday bustle. Only the lights at the base of the broad outside staircase and on either side of the second-floor entrance to the public rooms gave any hint of life behind the closed wrought iron gates.

Minx was waiting outside my kitchen door in the pissed-off pose she adopted when a meal was delayed one second past tummy time. I tossed her over my shoulder like a rag doll while I retrieved the note I'd left for Margo. When Minx had her little face stuck in her food bowl, I checked my answering machine for messages.

Margo: "Kel, I've got to take a rain check on the Bloody Mary. Paul and I have the flu."

Michael: "Mama, this weekend's been a total wipeout. I'm whipped and feel like crap. I can't shake this flu thing. I'm going to bed, catch you tomorrow."

Bed sounded good to me. I sloshed away the homestead grime and the lingering stench of Miss Lucinda's death in a long hot shower, filled a paper plate nestled in a wicker holder with an assortment of cheese and crackers, popped a Tab, plucked Agatha Christie's debut mystery, *The Mysterious Affair at Styles*, from my bedside bookcase—ignoring my tottering TBR pile for fear of causing an avalanche I was in no mood to pick up—and tucked myself in bed for a cozy evening of reading and telly. Minx settled herself opposite the cheese platter, the easier to snag nibbles when I had both hands occupied turning pages.

Monday morning I announced Miss Lucinda's death on the six o'clock news and dedicated the morning classics to her memory. I could think of nothing more fitting than a program of Elizabethan music performed by the Julian

Bream Consort. During a selection of pieces by John Dowland, the court lutenist to King Christian IV of Denmark from 1598 to 1606, I pondered the fate of Miss Lucinda's missing watch.

Was it the real thing? From what Miss Maude had said about Miss Lucinda's habits and having seen her house with my very own eyes, I couldn't imagine that Miss Lucinda would ever demean herself by wearing a piece of costume jewelry. I have a passion for fine jewelry—my knees go weak at the mere mention of Fabergé, but Cartier is certainly nothing to sneeze at—which far exceeds my resources but not my ability to look and appreciate. Although I'd never presumed to examine Miss Lucinda's watch closely, from afar it certainly looked like the real thing. Whether or not it had actually been a gift from the Prince of Wales was another matter entirely.

Where would one peddle such a treasure? It wasn't the type of object one could pawn. There are no pawn shops on St. Chris. Nor could I imagine anyone standing on Kongens Gade, flipping open a black raincoat and saying to wandering cruise ship passengers, "Wanna buy a hot watch cheap?" If I had that watch, first I'd want it appraised then possibly put up for auction. Christie's? Sotheby's? Offer it to Cartier?

There's a saying about life in a duty-free paradise: Luxuries are cheap, necessities are expensive. Putting it another way, we have one discount chain store where we pay through the nose for everything from toilet paper to televisions, but when it comes to jewelry? Isabeya is right up there with Michigan Avenue, Rodeo Drive, or Fifth Avenue. At much better prices. It was time to go on a field trip.

I headed to the Watering Hole for lunch and found the round table deserted.

"Where is everyone?" I asked when Carole brought me an iced tea.

"I think they're all home sick. Barbara came down for coffee and said Abby was out with the flu. No one's been in or out of Island Palms Real Estate all morning."

I decided to skip lunch. The Watering Hole was still short a chef and I wasn't in the mood to eat a burger by myself.

I walked into the first jewelry store. "Hi, Kelly," said the clerk. "Is this a look and drool day?" I was a frequent looker, but not much of a buyer.

"It's a look day, but I promise not to drool on your counters. Actually I was wondering if you had any reference books on antique jewelry I might look at."

"How antique?"

"Not very. Art Deco."

"I'll look in the manager's office. She's out sick today with the flu." The clerk returned a few minutes later. "She must have taken her books home with her. She sometimes does appraisal work over the weekend. Check back tomorrow or Wednesday."

"Buying a bauble, are we?"

I looked up to see Victoria standing next to me at the sapphire counter, where I was contemplating how many weeks I would have to eat hot dogs in order to pay for a sapphire and emerald pendant.

"Looking and drooling, Vic."

"I was so sorry to hear about Miss Lucinda. Do you have any idea what happened?"

I replied, "I understand it was natural causes," and bit my tongue before saying any more. If I admitted to being on the scene when another body was discovered on St. Chris, the island gossips would put me on the short list for the Jessica Fletcher Award.

"Let's go have a cup of tea and put our feet up. I've

been running around all morning." I followed Victoria out of the jewelry store. "On second thought, I don't want to go back to Dockside. The phone never stops ringing."

We headed for the Lime Tree, a recently opened lunch spot located in a courtyard a few doors away. We sat at a small round table on wire chairs that looked like they belonged in an ice cream parlor, and ordered iced tea.

"The first time my late husband Andrew and I came to St. Chris, as soon as people learned we were from England, we were told the story about Miss Lucinda and the Prince of Wales."

"Is it true, Vic?"

"Who can say? It was before my time, you know." Victoria smiled and stirred her tea. "The Duke of Windsor was quite a catch before the Duchess snared him. I daresay every young woman in England had her cap set for him when he was next in line for the throne. They all dreamed of becoming the Queen. Like in a fairy story."

"But do you think Miss Lucinda really knew him?"

"It's conceivable. I wouldn't be at all surprised. Especially if Miss Lucinda's family was known in court circles. If Mother were still alive, I'd write her and ask. She always kept up with the royal family. Growing up in America, you wouldn't know about that sort of thing."

"Only secondhand," I said. "One year I was in London when Parliament opened. I spent several chilly hours standing on the pavement, waiting to see Queen Elizabeth pass by in her coach. There was a charming little man next to me, as excited as a kid at Christmas. He was retired, but had worked as a deliveryman for a famous dress designer and once delivered a package to Buckingham Palace. Seeing the day through his eyes made it very special."

"Kelly, I think the kindest thing we can do for Miss Lucinda is to let the story stand without speculation. It doesn't hurt anyone; all the participants are gone. Part of this island's charm is never knowing if the next person you see on the street might be someone famous passing as an ordinary tourist. Pity the Queen of Denmark couldn't get away with it; she might have some fun here."

I sipped my tea. "Like Audrey Hepburn in the movie *Roman Holiday*?"

"Precisely."

I grinned. "It could be the other way around. Maybe the man who looks like a tourist is really a serial killer. Take that man over there . . ."

Victoria glanced at a man sitting across the courtyard with his back to us, bent over a newspaper. "Definitely a Jack the Ripper type," she said with a smile.

"Or Ted Bundy."

We giggled over our tea, but choked on our words when Chris Edwards rose from the table and headed our way with a broad smile on his face.

"Good afternoon, ladies. Kelly, are you all right? That's a nasty cough."

"Don't mind her, Chris," said Victoria. "Kelly was just saying that from the back you looked like Ted Bundy."

A fleeting frown crossed Chris's brow.

"We were only having a bit of fun, Chris," Victoria said. "We didn't know it was really you sitting over there until you stood up. Won't you join us?"

The smile returned to Chris's face. "Another time, Victoria. Right now I have matters to attend to concerning the royal visit. Call me about the wine order for the royal lunch. I'll have an answer later this afternoon. Kelly, you really should do something about that cough. What you need is bush tea. The governor swears by it."

My coughing fit prevented me from saying aloud, "The only thing the governor swears by comes in a bottle labeled 151 proof." But Chris had already left the restaurant.

# Chapter
# 22

"YO, MAMA. HOW was your weekend?" Michael reached out to hug me when I walked into the WBZE studio early Tuesday morning.

"Tiring. Construction is hard work. How are you feeling?"

"Not as good as you," he said with a leer, pulling me onto his lap.

Michael split promptly at six for his bedtime snack at McDonald's before going home to bed. He returned less than twenty minutes later with a take-out sack and a copy of Tuesday's *Coconut Telegraph*.

"Mama, I thought you might want some breakfast. I brought you a Sausage McMuffin and a copy of the morning paper. Did you know about this?" He waved the paper in front of me.

I glanced at the front page and nodded. Michael kissed me, then headed for the front door without saying another word. I unwrapped the McMuffin and nibbled while I read the paper.

The news of Miss Lucinda's passing was centered in a black-bordered box on the front page.

Lucinda Smythe-Chadworth, affectionately known as Miss Lucinda, died in her sleep on February sixth at her home in Estate Rose Hill. Miss Lucinda, born in England, came to St. Chris as a bride in 1928 and was the widow of Planter Ian Chadworth. She was active throughout her life in community affairs, and was best known for her untiring efforts on behalf of the St. Chris hospital. She was also the social columnist for this paper for many years. Miss Lucinda is survived by many friends, including her longtime friend and companion Maude Rasmussen. Services will be held Friday at one P.M. at the Anglican Church in Isabeya, with burial immediately following in the Isabeya cemetery. In lieu of flowers, it is requested that donations be made to the St. Chris hospital.

To the right of the obituary was a very flattering formal portrait of Miss Lucinda, taken thirty years or so prior to her death. I remembered Margo telling me that in her youth Miss Lucinda had been a real beauty. Seeing the photograph made it very easy to imagine Miss Lucinda as a young woman on the arm of the Prince of Wales.

I made a mental note to call Dahlia's, the local florist, when she opened at nine-thirty to order a suitable arrangement for delivery to the church on Friday, then pulled my personal checkbook out of my tote bag. I was making out a check to the St. Chris hospital when the phone rang.

"Good morning, WBZE."

"Hi, Kelly. You sound distracted. Did I call at the wrong time?"

"Hey, Benjamin. I'm making out a check to the hospital. I just finished reading Miss Lucinda's obituary in the *Telegraph*."

"Don't believe everything you read in the *Telegraph*."

I laughed. "I never do. Does anyone? Which part shouldn't I believe this time?"

"The part about dying in her sleep."

"I knew that. She choked to death on her own vomit, but you can't put that on the front page of the *Telegraph*."

"There may be more to it than the flu, Kelly."

"Benjamin, what are you saying?"

"Nothing right now. Dr. Williams hasn't finished his examination. But I'm asking you to keep your mouth shut."

"Should I take that request personally?"

Benjamin chuckled. "Not really. I said the same thing to Camille, Amelia, and Miss Maude."

Miss Maude was my next caller. "I hope I'm not disturbing you while you're on the air."

"Not at all." I checked the airtime remaining on *Horowitz in Moscow*, the featured album for the first hour of the morning classics. Vladimer Horowitz was spellbinding his audience with Chopin's "Mazurka in C Sharp Minor." "I'm good for another ten minutes."

"I wonder if I might impose upon your free time this afternoon."

"Of course you can. What can I do for you?"

"I need to go over to Lucy's house to select suitable clothing for her burial and I thought you might assist me."

"I'd be glad to."

"And then I have an appointment this afternoon at three with Father James at the Anglican church to finalize the arrangements for Lucy's funeral service. You will be there on Friday, won't you? The service begins at one."

"I wouldn't miss it." Bad choice of words. I sounded like I was RSVP-ing to a party invitation. "I'm sorry, Miss

Maude, that's not what I meant to say. Of course I'll be at the funeral."

"That's quite all right, dear. I fully understood your meaning. Shall we say one o'clock this afternoon at Lucy's house?"

I looked down at my tank top, shorts, and flip-flops. They were okay for going through Miss Lucinda's closet, but not for making funeral arrangements at the church. I would have to skip lunch, fly home to change clothes, and burn rubber to get to Miss Lucinda's house on time. "I can make one o'clock."

"I am very grateful, Kelly. I'll see you at one."

At three minutes past one I pulled up in front of Miss Lucinda's house, suitably attired for the occasion in leather sandals, a wrap skirt, and the tank top I'd worn to work.

Miss Maude once again stood at the top of the welcoming arms staircase, but this time she was talking to another woman, a few years younger than Miss Lucinda.

"Kelly, I'd like you to meet Elodia, Lucy's longtime friend and housekeeper."

We shook hands and I saw that Elodia had been crying.

"Oh Miss Maude, poor Miss Lucy," she wailed. "Had I known she be so sick, I never leave her. You know I always take good care of my Miss Lucy."

Miss Maude put her arm around Elodia's bony shoulders. "Lucy always said she couldn't do without you. You were her treasure." She reached into her pocketbook for a neatly folded tissue, which she passed to Elodia. "Now dry your eyes and then perhaps you'd make us a pot of tea and bring it to Lucy's bedroom. We'll need three cups."

Elodia headed for the kitchen, wiping her eyes and sniffling with every step.

Miss Maude and I walked through the house to Miss

Lucinda's bedroom. Boudoir would have been a more apt description. Except for the antique mahogany four-poster bed and matching clothes press, everything in the room was pink. The plastered walls, the tray ceiling, the carpet on the floor, the curtains, the chintzes on the chairs, the sheets, pillowcases, and coverlet on the bed, even the bulbs in the lamps. All pink. I felt as if I'd plunged head-first into a vat of cotton candy.

Miss Maude put her pocketbook on the chair next to Miss Lucinda's dressing table, then walked briskly to the clothes press and opened the double doors. Inside were Miss Lucinda's dresses and an assortment of shoes that would have turned Imelda Marcos green with envy.

"Lucy did love shoes," said Miss Maude, reaching for the new pair of cerise leather pumps with the straps across the insteps. "She never could resist a shoe sale. I think these will do nicely."

I pointed to a pink print silk dress hanging on a pink padded hanger. "What about that dress? It's the one she wore to dinner at your house. She looked lovely in it and it goes with the shoes."

"A wise choice," said Miss Maude, lifting the hanger off the rod. She laid the dress and shoes on the bed as Elodia entered the room with a tea tray. "I think we'll take tea on the front gallery; it's much cooler there. There's such a nice breeze today."

We followed behind Elodia to the front gallery. When tea had been poured and biscuits served, Elodia said to Miss Maude, "Miss Lucy is going to be very upset. One of her best glasses has gone missing."

"Show me." Miss Maude followed Elodia back toward the kitchen. I trailed a few paces behind them.

The walls of the kitchen were lined with old-fashioned glass-fronted cabinets. "When I reach for the tea things, I see this is not right." Elodia pointed to a cabinet where an assortment of cut crystal was arranged in rows by height and shape. "You know Miss Lucy was very particular. She have twelve of everything and she make me wash and dry each piece by hand."

The squat cocktail glasses were in the front of the cupboard, slightly above eye level, arranged precisely like little soldiers in two rows of six. Elodia pointed to a gap in the middle of the second row. "It was not that way when I left on Saturday. I took a glass from the front"—she pointed to the right end of the front row—"and put it on a little silver tray, like I always do for Miss Lucy, with a bowl of the fancy nuts she liked."

"Nuts? There were nuts in that bowl? I thought it was Easter candy," I said.

"Miss Lucy was very fond of Jordan almonds. They bring them in special at the market just for her," said Elodia with a curt nod.

"And where did you put the tray?" I asked, careful not to make a simple question sound like a third degree.

"In Miss Lucy's sitting room. Unless she expecting company, I always take it to the sitting room."

"Was she expecting company on Saturday?" I asked.

Elodia shook her head. "She would have told me so I could put out something to eat. Miss Lucy never let her guests go without something in their stomachs."

"Lucy telephoned me about three-thirty," said Miss Maude. "She said she'd just gotten up from her nap and the heat had given her a little headache. She said she was staying home Saturday night and would see me for church Sunday morning."

"Miss Lucy was her happy self when I left at four," said Elodia. "She was in the sitting room with her picture books and humming a little tune under her breath. Like this." Elodia began humming tunelessly, "Da de dah dah dah dah. Da de dah d-a-a-h dah dah. Dah dah d-a-a-h dah d-e-e dah dah. Dah dah d-a-a-h dah d-e-e dah dah."

If there was a melody lurking there, I sure as hell wasn't able to discern it and I used to win every time we played an underwater version of "Name That Tune" at summer camp. "Was there a name to that song?" I asked.

"Miss Lucy never say. But she always hum so when she was very happy about something." Elodia turned to stare into the cupboard again. "I sure wish I knew what become of that glass."

"Perhaps Lucy broke the glass herself and said nothing about it," said Miss Maude, patting Elodia's shoulder. "I'll see that the glass is replaced and the set made complete. Come, let us have our tea. Then I need you to get some undergarments for Lucy and pack them with the shoes and dress I've put out on her bed."

We stopped at the funeral parlor to drop off Miss Lucinda's clothes before heading for the Anglican church.

While we waited for Father James in the church office, I asked Miss Maude what would become of Rose Hill and all its lovely furnishings.

"Lucy was very shrewd when it came to money matters," said Miss Maude. "Everything she had—except for her personal effects and jewelry, which come to me—was placed in a trust, of which I am the surviving trustee, to benefit the St. Chris hospital. The house and its contents will become a public museum, and Elodia will continue to live in the house as a life tenant at the same salary she received when she worked for Lucy."

"Who runs the St. Chris hospital?" I asked.

"The government, of course."

"Ladies, I do apologize for keeping you waiting," said Father James as he entered the church office dressed in slacks and an open-collared shirt. "Please forgive my appearance. The clergy are allowed to play free at the golf club on Tuesday afternoons." He took both of Miss

Maude's hands in his. "Maude, I am so sorry about Lucy. She has been in my prayers ever since I heard the sad news."

We spent an hour with Father James arranging Miss Lucinda's funeral. Benjamin, Freddy, and Elodia's son-in-law Rupert would serve as pallbearers. "Christopher Edwards called yesterday afternoon from Government House to offer his services if needed. I said I would consult with you first and let him know."

"Dear Christopher," said Miss Maude. "Please thank him for me and say I accept his generous offer. I think Lucy would have approved."

"Will there be a viewing?"

"Yes," said Miss Maude. "Thursday evening from seven until nine."

"And a reception after the burial? The church women would be happy to take care of that here if you like."

"Victoria has already offered to have it at Dockside," said Miss Maude.

"Well, then, I think we have everything in order. I will begin preparing Miss Lucinda's eulogy."

The bell was tolling four-thirty as Miss Maude and I left Father James's office.

# Chapter
## 23

"KEL, WHERE IN the hell have you been?" groused Margo as I slid into my chair for Wednesday lunch at the Watering Hole.

"I've been to London to see the Queen."

"What? What are you going on about? Forget I asked."

"Fine welcome, sweetie. You must be feeling better. You're always so agreeable when you're sick."

"Sick? You don't want to know how sick I was. I didn't stop whoopsing for two days. I thought I was going to die. Oh God, Kel, I'm sorry."

"About what?"

"Miss Lucinda. I didn't see a paper until this morning. The obit said she died in her sleep. At least you weren't around when her body was found. Pretty soon people are going to start calling you Jessica Fletcher."

I bit my tongue when I heard Benjamin's voice clanging in my head like a fire bell. Instead I smiled sweetly and said, "I'm glad you're feeling better. I missed you."

Carole stopped by the table to put a tall iced tea in

front of me and said, "The special today is spaghetti with garlic bread. All you can eat."

Margo groaned. "Don't mention garlic. What's the soup?"

"Hot minestrone or cold gazpacho."

"Huh? Who comes up with these things?"

"The new chef is a vegetarian."

"There's a new chef?" I said. "Since when?"

"Yesterday afternoon."

"Well, he won't last long with this crowd of meat eaters," said Margo.

Carole looked over her shoulder, then said in a low voice, "He is a she."

"Carole, I don't care if she's an alien raised by androids in a biosphere. If she can't put out a decent burger, she's whole-grain toast. Read my lips on that one. What are my chances of getting scrambled eggs for lunch?"

"Slim to none, Margo. The chef is allergic to eggs. Let me know when you're ready to order." Carole split for the bar.

"Drink up, Kel. We're outta here. Let's go to Port in a Storm."

"There's a new place in town. The Lime Tree. Vic and I stopped there the other day."

"Lead the way."

Margo and I sat at the same table, on the same wire chairs that Vic and I had occupied. Margo looked around the courtyard and nodded her approval. "This place is really charming. It should do very well. Provided it attracts the locals." It was a reality of doing business in St. Chris that most new places did well during the winter high-tourist season, but unless they kept local business through the slow off-season months, the out-of-business sign would be up by fall. "You know what I want first, Kel? A Bloody Mary. Join me?"

I had nothing on my dance card for the afternoon. "Why not? Sounds good."

The Bloodys were served in glasses the size of small vases, loaded with ice and garnished with a freshly cut wedge of key lime, probably plucked from the lime trees growing on the premises. I sipped my drink. "This is good. No aquavit." Margo smiled. "Tell me about dinner at Jerry's. I hated to miss it, but I was pooped from working on the homestead house."

"You didn't miss much, except for the wine. Jerry made his three-cheese lasagna with the chunky meat sauce and served it with a really great burgundy. I asked him where he got it—it's the most expensive bottle I've ever seen in his house and I know he didn't pay retail—but he wouldn't tell me. The poop. I think he's trying to hoard it all for himself. Unfortunately we never got to dessert. And Heidi made deep-dish apple pie, which Paul just loves."

"What happened?"

"Damned flu bug. Abby said she wasn't feeling too hot when she arrived. By the time we'd eaten the lasagna, we were all lining up for the john. You know Jerry's house. He's only got one bathroom. Paul and I got the hell out of there and went home. I guess Heidi got stuck doing the dishes that night."

"How come?"

"She was the only one who didn't get sick. But then, she had the flu a couple of weeks ago and wasn't eating or drinking much. I guess once you've had the flu, you don't get it again." Margo stopped talking long enough to polish off most of her drink. "Hand me a menu, will you?"

We sat looking at the menus in silence for a couple of minutes. Margo let hers drop to the table and put her hand on her stomach. "Kel, I've gotta take a pass on lunch. I think I got out of bed too soon. Pay for my drink, will you?" She picked up her purse and ran out of the restaurant.

The waiter came to the table with our bar tab and a worried expression on his face. "Was something wrong with the drinks?"

"No, my friend had the flu last weekend and she's still not over it." I laid a generous tip on top of the bar bill.

"There's a lot of flu going around these days. I hope you'll come back when your friend is better."

"You can count on it." I drained my glass and left the Lime Tree. It was the third day in a row I hadn't had lunch. I decided to head for home and a roast beef sandwich on homemade cheddar-chive bread. Then I'd spend the afternoon lazing on my gallery reading *The Mysterious Affair at Styles*.

# Chapter
# 24

MISS MAUDE ASKED if I would do her a special favor and meet her at the funeral home at 6 P.M. Thursday to make sure everything was in order for the viewing beginning at seven.

"I hate to impose on you further, Kelly, but Amelia and Camille are at school all day and have families to feed before they can get ready themselves."

Like a wimp I agreed. Even though spending Thursday evening at a funeral home was not my idea of a good time. I was hoping to make a brief appearance and head for home. Why is it women with children get all the breaks?

"I certainly don't expect you to stay until nine," Miss Maude added. "I know you retire early in order to get up early for work."

I pawed through my closet for suitable clothing. I was saving my white dress for the funeral itself. I hadn't worn it in almost a year, since the last time I went to a funeral, but it still fit. In St. Chris women wear white to a funeral instead of black. Don't ask me why, that's just how it is. I put the dress with its matching shoes and purse in a garment bag to take to the station with me Friday morning. I wouldn't have time to run home to change when my shift was over at noon and still get to the funeral on time.

What to wear to the viewing? It was one of those dreaded in-between occasions, not casual and not formal. I hate those. I really don't have the clothes for them. My wardrobe goes from shorts and tank tops to long skirts and formal black with very little in between. If I were Abby, I'd have a closet full of suits that would be perfect for any occasion, and Margo the clothes horse always knew what to wear down to the last accessory.

I pulled a simple navy cotton knit dress with a matching belt. It would do in a pinch. I found a navy purse and matching espadrilles in my closet. Then I raided my floor safe for my favorite jade jewelry. Jade pendant on a long gold chain, jade segment bracelet paired with one in plain gold, simple gold hoops. I grabbed the garment bag and tossed it in the back of my car so I wouldn't forget it Friday morning, and left the house at five-thirty, driving into the blinding setting sun.

I arrived at the funeral parlor west of Isabeya as Miss Maude was pulling into the parking lot in her Land Rover. We parked side by side and entered the building together.

Miss Lucinda was laid out in a rosewood casket, lined with pale pink satin, wearing the dress and shoes Miss Maude and I had selected two days earlier. She looked so natural I expected her to sit up and ask for a rum swizzle or a glass of gin.

"Lucy looks lovely," Miss Maude said to Mr. Richard, the funeral director. "You've done a good job, although there's a bit more rouge on her cheeks than she would have liked. Lucy was very sparing when it came to cosmetics."

I looked at Miss Lucinda's hands, white gloved and crossed decorously above her ample waist. "Miss Maude," I said softly, "what became of Miss Lucinda's wedding rings? I know she was wearing them when she died."

"Not to worry, dear. Dr. Williams removed them and sent them to me."

I glanced again at Miss Lucinda before turning to sign the guest register. I was halfway across the room when I made a U-turn and headed back to the open casket.

"Miss Maude, please come here for a minute."

Miss Maude excused herself and came to stand at my side. "What is it, Kelly?"

I pointed to Miss Lucinda's left wrist. There, fastened to her wrist and almost hidden by her white cotton glove, was her missing watch.

"Where did this come from?" Miss Maude asked Mr. Richard.

"I don't know. It must have been with the clothes you brought."

"No, I'm certain it wasn't," Miss Maude said firmly.

I reached for Miss Lucinda's wrist to remove the watch.

"Wait!" said Mr. Richard. "I will assist you." He pulled a pen knife from his pocket. A tightly tied string ran from the back of the watchband under the glove and was looped around the middle finger of Miss Lucinda's left hand. He smiled apologetically as he cut the string. "There have been occasions in the past when a loved one's jewelry has come up missing after a viewing. We try to take every precaution." He handed the watch to Miss Maude.

"Will you excuse us for a moment?" Miss Maude asked Mr. Richard. He backed away from us to stand at attention next to the guest register.

Miss Maude and I looked at the watch together. I

glanced at my own watch, then at Miss Lucinda's. I motioned to Mr. Richard. "When was this watch put on Miss Lucinda's wrist?"

"Yesterday afternoon when we dressed her. Why? Is something wrong?"

"No, I was just curious. Thank you. We'll be with you in a minute."

Mr. Richard returned to his post at the guest register.

"Miss Maude," I whispered, "we need to get this watch to a jeweler to have it appraised."

"Why, Kelly? That's definitely Lucy's watch. I've seen it on her wrist every day of her life. I'd recognize it anywhere."

"Miss Maude, this watch is a fake."

"Kelly, no. It can't be. Why would you say such a thing?"

I took Miss Lucinda's watch and held it next to my own. They were both keeping perfect time.

"My watch has a quartz movement. It never loses a second. Miss Lucinda's watch also has a quartz movement. If it were the real one, it would have stopped by now. A watch made in the 1920s needs to be wound every single day."

Miss Maude's eyes widened. A frown creased her forehead, then a small smile played on her lips. "Lucy would have been very grateful to you, Kelly. She always admired your sleuthing skills." Miss Maude dropped the watch in her handbag. "I will take the watch to the jeweler in the morning. For now we will say no more about it to anyone."

We took our places beside Mr. Richard to greet the new arrivals.

# Chapter
## 25

I WALKED INTO WBZE Friday morning with the garment bag slung over my shoulder.

"What's with the glad rags, Mama? Got a hot date today?"

"With a cold corpse," I replied. In answer to Michael's questioning stare, I added, "Miss Lucinda's funeral is this afternoon and I won't have time to go home and change."

"Jesus. I forgot all about that. Do you want me to go with you?" I knew from Michael's tone that the answer he expected was "yes" but he'd be much happier if I said "no."

"Only if singing eight verses of six different hymns is your idea of a fun way to spend a Friday afternoon."

"I think I'll take a pass. Is that okay with you?"

"You really didn't know Miss Lucinda. It's okay. You need your beauty rest." I left the studio to stash the clothes in my office.

Michael trailed behind me. "What do you say we blow this place tomorrow morning when I'm off the air? I've got backstage passes for an SRO rock festival concert in San Juan Saturday night."

"Michael, I can't. I promised Benjamin I'd help finish the homestead house this weekend. The Queen arrives here exactly one week from tomorrow."

Michael put his arms around me and began tickling my right earlobe with his tongue. "Think of it, Mama. Room service, lazy time on the beach, a little action in the casino, the concert up close and personal. There's a big bash with the band afterwards. We can have champagne brunch in our room Sunday morning."

I sighed. "I wish I could. But a promise is a promise. Ask me another time."

Michael dropped his arms to his sides. "Mama, there never is a another time. I've been trying to get you off the rock since last September. And something always comes up."

"I don't call a force-five hurricane 'something,' " I said.

"Forget it." Michael headed back to the studio.

I hate it when guys get that injured tone in their voices. And why did Michael have to wait until the last minute to spring this weekend jaunt on me? A little advance warning would have been nice. But I meant what I said, and it wasn't just an excuse, I *had* promised Benjamin I'd help finish the homestead house.

Michael left the station the minute he cued his sign-off, "Thanks for the Memories." I called out, "Have fun this weekend" from the music room, where I was pulling albums for my show, but I don't think he heard me over the sound of the front door slamming shut.

Miss Lucinda's funeral was an SRO event in itself. By the time the service began a few minutes after one, the Anglican church was packed elbow to elbow in the pews and latecomers were standing in the doorways to pay tribute to a much-loved lady.

I sat in a front pew with Elodia, her daughter Hester, and son-in-law Rupert, one of Miss Lucinda's pallbearers. Also sitting in the front pews were Miss Maude, Amelia and Freddy, Camille and Benjamin, Dr. Williams, and Chris Edwards.

I wasn't exaggerating when I'd told Michael there would be six hymns with eight verses each. The service had already been running for over an hour by the time Father James began the eulogy. The funeral parlor had given out cardboard memorial fans, mounted on flat sticks resembling tongue depressors, to the women as they entered the church. The fans were flipping back and forth in the still air, mingling the scents of spicy aftershaves and floral perfumes into a headache-inducing, throat-gagging musk. I tried to ignore it, but the afternoon heat combined with the musk and scents of the funeral wreaths was making me a little giddy. The fans were stilled when women reached in their purses for handkerchiefs and tissues to dry their eyes at the end of the eulogy.

Miss Lucinda's funeral service ended two hours and fifteen minutes after it had begun. When the pallbearers were at last carrying the closed casket from the church, I almost lost it. As I watched Benjamin, Freddy, Rupert, and Chris leaving the church in lockstep, the only thing that kept flitting through my head was the song "Heigh-Ho" from Disney's *Snow White*. I felt Elodia stiffen slightly beside me. I dug the nails of my index fingers into the pads of my thumbs in order to stifle the giggle welling in my chest and stared straight ahead, with as much solemnity as I could muster, at the masses of flowers lining the altar.

The funeral goers filed out of the Anglican church to the sound of the tolling bell for the trek to the burial in the Isabeya cemetery two blocks behind the church.

The public cemetery dates back to the late 1600s and

is located on the southwestern corner of the six-by-six-
block grid that comprises Isabeya. When the Danes rebuilt
Isabeya after the 1764 town fire, the cemetery was one of
the few reference points still standing. The cemetery itself
is divided by narrow roads, formerly cart paths, into sec-
tions according to religious affiliation. Miss Lucinda
would be interred in the Anglican section next to her late
husband, Planter Ian Chadwick. Walking through the
cemetery and reading the stones is a crash course in St.
Chris history. Many stones tell of journeys taken and
dreams unfulfilled. Of suffering patients who came to St.
Chris for the health-restoring climate, only to die on ship-
board in the harbor before disembarking. There are also
private burial grounds on St. Chris in the ruins of the old
sugar plantations, and one graveyard that tourists never
see or hear of on the site of the former leper colony.

Instead of proceeding directly to the Isabeya Cemetery,
we followed the hearse on foot through town as is the
local custom when someone prominent dies. Down the
length of Kongens Gade to Government House, along
Kirke Gade one block to Dronningens Gade, and westward along Dronningens Gade until we reached the cemetery. Hanging on almost every door were black wreaths
or ribbons to mark Miss Lucinda's passing. The flag at
Government House was lowered to half-mast. The mourners walked slowly past windows and doors tightly shuttered to keep the spirit of the dead from entering.

Forty-five minutes at the cemetery and Miss Lucinda
was finally laid to rest.

I looked at my watch. Four-thirty. Time to head to
Dockside for the funeral meats.

I'd parked in the fort parking lot, much closer to Dockside than the Anglican church, making it easier to get
home later. For the third time that day I hoofed along
Kongens Gade, wishing I'd worn pantyhose with my

closed-in shoes because I now had blisters the size of political campaign buttons on both heels of my aching feet. Every step I took was pure agony.

Victoria had put out quite a spread. There were cut crystal bowls the size of washbasins filled with rum punch or nonalcoholic fruit punch; and platters of ham, turkey, bread, cheese, and fruit running the length of the buffet. On each table were small plates of petit fours and bowls of Jordan almonds.

I quickly found an empty seat and gingerly eased off my shoes. I didn't care if I had to crawl to my car on my hands and knees, no way were those shoes going back on my feet.

"May we join you?" I looked up to see Benjamin and Dr. Williams standing with full plates.

"Please do," I said.

"Aren't you eating, Kelly?" said Benjamin.

"In a minute," I said, wiggling my toes under the table to get the circulation going. "You don't know what a relief it is to finally take my shoes off."

Benjamin grinned as he removed his suit jacket and loosened his tie. "Yes, I think I do."

When everyone at our table had finished eating and refilled their cups with rum punch, Benjamin turned to me. "Dr. Williams wants to tell us what he discovered."

"Actually, it was you, young lady, who gave me the idea of what to look for. I thank you for that."

"For what?" I said. "What did I do?"

"Miss Lucy, may she rest in peace, had a drinking problem. In fact, not to mince words, she was a confirmed alcoholic. Which is not uncommon on this island, where liquor is cheap, social drinking is encouraged, and there are too many people with too much time on their hands and too little to do. She wasn't always that way. In her younger years . . ." Dr. Williams sighed in reminiscence.

"In her younger years, Miss Lucy was a real go-getter. But after her husband died, she lost some of her zest."

"And turned to drinking?"

"She always drank socially, but she began drinking more and more privately. I tried to get her to quit, or at least cut back, after an ulcer attack put her in the hospital. Her liver was deteriorating to the point of cirrhosis. Miss Lucy hadn't much longer to live, perhaps three months at the outside, before her liver failed. It's a blessing she was spared that suffering. But it wasn't her liver that killed her." Dr. Williams paused, looked over Benjamin's shoulder, and said, "Hello, Chris. Was there something you wanted?"

I looked up to see Chris standing at Benjamin's elbow. "Ben, may I have a word with you about the royal visit?"

We were interrupted by the sound of beepers beeping like a chorus of crazed canaries. Benjamin, Dr. Williams, and Chris reached in their pockets. "That's mine," said Dr. Williams. "And mine," said Benjamin. "Mine, too," said Chris.

Before the dust had settled in the wake of the men's departures, I reached for my shoes and headed for the fort parking lot. Blissfully barefoot.

# Chapter
# 26

MY FEET STILL hurt on Saturday morning and my heels looked like raw meat. I covered each heel with a triple stripe of Band-Aids before slipping on my workday Reef flip-flops. What would the Queen think if I wore sandals to the royal dinner? She probably wouldn't care one way or the other—when in Rome and all that—but Miss Maude would consider it a social gaffe. At least we'd be sitting during most of the dinner, while the invitees to the royal garden party would be standing for the better part of two hours in the queue to meet the Queen. Since I hadn't received an invitation to the garden party, I could pamper my feet until the royal dinner.

The fairground was deserted except for the homestead house building crew. The grounds and fair buildings were ready for final preparation Thursday night when the midway rides would be installed. On Friday night the school exhibits would be set up and the vendors would bring in their wares. The church ladies would be awake most of Friday night into Saturday morning busily cooking kallaloo, frying johnnycakes, and frosting multilayered cakes.

The building crew finished construction early Saturday afternoon, then prepped the house for painting, working from the roof down. By five o'clock the house had its first exterior coat of paint drying in the late-afternoon sun. We stashed our tools, paint cans, and drop cloths inside the house until the final coat of paint was applied on Sunday.

Benjamin and I were the last to leave the work site. "It's looking good, Kelly. I never thought we'd get this done on time." He flipped the ring of door keys in the air and caught them in his hand. "Got time for a beer on your way home? Before we left Dockside yesterday, Chris asked if I'd drop off a key at Government House. He wants to have it gold-plated for the Queen to use at the dedication next Saturday."

I looked down at my ragged paint-spattered shorts. "A beer sounds good. As long as we go someplace without a dress code."

We ended up at Dockside's Lower Deck. While Benjamin ran across Kongens Gade to Government House to drop off the homestead house key, I headed for the loo to wash the paint off my hands.

I sat at a table on the waterfront sipping a cold Heineken, watching sailboats tie up at moorings for the night, seeing lights come on in the little hip-roofed West Indian–style houses on the hillsides, looking at the restored gazebo on the town green next to the fort, and finally glancing at the freshly painted flagpole where the Dannebrog would once again be raised to welcome Queen Margrethe and Prince Henrik.

"Where's my beer?"

"Still on ice. I didn't want it to get warm. What took you so long?"

"I had a devil of a time finding Chris. I thought he'd

be waiting for me, I called him from my car phone as we left the fairground."

Benjamin downed half his beer in one swallow; "You want something to eat?"

I shook my head. "I'll wait until I get home."

"You and Michael have plans tonight?"

I shook my head again. "He went to San Juan for a rock concert." I leaned forward in my chair. "Benjamin, can we talk? I'm worried about something."

"I'm not very good at that sort of thing, Kelly. Maybe you'd better talk to Camille."

"Benjamin, you're the last person I would ever confuse with 'Dear Abby.' This isn't personal."

Relief flooded Benjamin's face. "Oh. In that case, go ahead."

"I was thinking about our conversation with Dr. Williams after Miss Lucinda's funeral."

"What about it?"

"It didn't make sense. Why was Dr. Williams thanking me? What really killed Miss Lucinda?"

"I don't know. I haven't been able to talk to Dr. Williams since the funeral."

The church bell tolled six. Benjamin looked at his watch, confirming the time. "Oh, Lord," he said, downing the last of his beer, "Camille is going to kill me. We're going out for dinner tonight and I promised her I'd be home by six. We'll have to continue this conversation another time."

I didn't talk to Benjamin again until Sunday afternoon at the fairground. By the time he arrived, the roof and outside walls had their second coat of paint and we were getting ready to stain the interior walls and floors.

"Fine bomba you turned out to be," I said, using the old cane worker term for field boss. "We've been busting our backs out here in the hot sun for hours. I hope you brought the beer."

The rest of the building crew laughed. Maubi said, "Don't you worry, Morning Lady, I got plenty cold ones in my van for when we get this job finished."

Benjamin motioned me over to him and said quietly, "I spent the morning at the hospital with Doc Williams."

"What did he have to say?" I couldn't wait to hear Benjamin's reply.

"He hasn't said anything. Dr. Williams was in a car accident last night and is in critical condition."

# Chapter
## 27

I WAS TOO shocked to do anything but stare at Benjamin.

"He was involved in a single-car accident on his way home from the hospital. The car mashed into a guardrail on the north shore road. He lives not far from Miss Maude, you know."

I shook my head. "I didn't know."

"People drive too fast on that road. We put up speed signs and warn people about the curves, but there's not much traffic at night and they drive like it's the last lap of the Indy 500."

"When did the accident happen?"

"Sometime last night. We don't patrol that road much at night because there aren't many homes along there. A patrol car passed this morning and found Dr. Williams unconscious in his car, slumped over the steering wheel. His head must have broken the windshield. That Volkswagen Beetle of his is so old it doesn't even have seatbelts, but he loves that car and won't buy a new one." Benjamin shook his head sadly.

I put my hand on Benjamin's arm. "Poor Dr. Williams. What a loss this would be for St. Chris. And his family."

"Dr. Williams is a widower. His wife died twenty-some years ago. I always thought he was sweet on Miss Lucy. They would have made a good pair. I've got to get back to the hospital. I'll let you know if there's any change in his condition."

I sent up a prayer for the man whose quick thinking had saved me from almost certain death less than a year ago, then spent the rest of the afternoon on my knees staining the homestead house gallery floor.

We ended the day sitting on the ground around Maubi's van drinking the cold ones he'd put on ice in a cooler. The late-afternoon sun shone through the open windows of the homestead house, filling it with golden light, making it look warm and inviting.

I picked up my beer and walked around the outside of the house to stand in the little lean-to kitchen, wondering what it must have been like to cook on a coal pot, and prepare meals without refrigeration. Like living on St. Chris after Hurricane Gilda, I said to myself, smiling at the thought. I heard the sound of footsteps shuffling through the dirt and looked to see Maubi standing in the kitchen doorway.

"For a second it look to me like my grandmama Alveena come back from the dead," he said, rubbing his eyes. "She raise five children in a little bitty house just like this. They had a big vegetable garden, lots of fruit trees and some avocado pear, a little plot of sugar cane, a few chickens, a couple cows, and some goats. Everybody eat good and nobody fuss about foolishness like hundred-dollar tennis shoes or wanting to better their neighbors. It's like I say to you after the storm, Morning Lady—hard times make strong people. The same was true for my grandmama and it be true for us now. Only the weak think they entitle to lime before they sweat."

I smiled when I realized Maubi had just told me the St. Chris version of the fable about the grasshopper and the ant.

"Come. I got another cold one waiting for you." Maubi put his arm around me to ease the weight on his bum leg and we walked back to his van in the fading light of the setting sun.

# Chapter
# 28

DR. WILLIAMS DIED Sunday night, less than twenty-four hours after his accident.

"He never regained consciousness, Kelly. Even if he wanted to talk, it would have been no use trying. He broke his jaw on the steering wheel when his head hit the windshield."

I thanked Benjamin for calling and went to bed feeling very sad.

For the second Monday in a row, I began my broadcast with a death announcement. In Dr. Williams's memory I aired—uninterrupted by commercials, chat, or station ID breaks—one of his favorite classical pieces, Leonard Bernstein's May 1964 recording of Beethoven's *Ninth Symphony*.

During the seventy-minute concert, I thought about Dr. Williams and how much he had meant to St. Chris. For almost fifty years he'd practiced tropical medicine, coming back to St. Chris after World War II because he'd been stationed here at the long-defunct submarine base during the war. He could have made a hell of a lot more money someplace else, but he once told me that on St. Chris he could make a difference, whereas in the States he'd be just another pill pusher with six-figure ulcers. In that respect he was like every other expatriate in paradise who chose to make St. Chris home. We all came the first time for the weather and stayed—or went home, then came back permanently—because we couldn't get the sand out of our shoes or the easygoing people and the laid-back St. Chris lifestyle out of our heads. As Margo put it so succinctly one night after she'd had a couple of frozen margaritas, "It ain't the money that's important, honey. If your life sucks, who cares if you're rich?" I say amen to that.

I toddled off to the Watering Hole for lunch.

"Hey, Kelly," said Carole. "We're having a special today. Fourteen percent off anything on the menu that's red. You wanna start with a Bloody Mary?"

"What is this?" I asked. "Another Danish thing? You're really pushing the envelope on that one."

"Get a grip, Kelly. It's Valentine's Day."

Gulp. I just know my face turned as red as a cinnamon candy heart.

"What's the matter, Kel?" said Margo. "Are you having a hot flash?"

"Bite your tongue, witch." I turned back to Carole. "I'd love a Bloody. Made with vodka, not aquavit."

"We got a lot of aquavit to peddle," said Carole. "I can't understand why the Danish Mary isn't selling better." Carole dropped a menu on the table, then headed for the bar.

"Margo, I feel like an ass. I completely forgot about Valentine's Day. I didn't buy Michael a card or a present or anything."

"Kel, guys are supposed to buy you presents."

"All right, smarty. Tell me what you did for Paul."

Margo leaned over and whispered in my ear.

"You did *what*?"

Margo grinned.

*"Really?"*

She nodded.

"What was Paul's reaction?"

Margo shook her fingers as if she'd seared them on a hot griddle.

"That good. Tell me." I leaned over to whisper in Margo's ear. "Where did you get the underwear?"

Margo whispered back.

"No kidding," I said. "I didn't know they carried that sort of stuff."

"In the back. You have to ask for it."

"I'm heading over there right after lunch," I said.

"Where are you going?" said Jerry, joining the table.

"Uh, the card shop. I forgot to buy Michael a Valentine. What did you get Heidi?"

"A heart-shaped box of candy. It's what I give her every year."

"What? No red roses?" said Margo. "Jerry, you're *so* romantic."

"When was the last time you priced roses? They jacked the price up to seventy-five dollars a dozen for Valentine's Day. Candy's cheaper and it lasts longer."

"I thought Heidi didn't like chocolate," said Abby, setting her briefcase under her chair before sitting down.

"She doesn't. But I do. She gets to keep the box."

Only Carole's arrival with a tray full of Bloody Marys saved Jerry from being lynched on the spot.

"Hey, Jerry. I understand I missed a great dinner at your place a week ago. Margo said the wine was superb."

"It was nothing special. Just a bottle I found lying around the house." Jerry picked up his white-on-white and took a healthy swallow. "How's the homestead house coming along?"

"Great. We finished it yesterday. All we've got left to do is put in the furnishings Thursday night."

The impending royal visit filled the rest of the lunch conversation.

"Have you decided what to wear, Kel?" asked Margo.

"I think so, but I may change my mind." I was too embarrassed to tell anyone I hadn't been invited to the garden party.

"Why don't you come to Sea Breezes on Saturday to change? Then we can all go together. It'll be easier to park if we only take one car."

"It might be better if I meet you in town. I'm going to be at the fairground most of the morning."

"If you change your mind, the invitation stands."

After lunch I headed off to Margo's secret shop, then went home to plan a Valentine surprise for Michael.

# Chapter
# 29

I SET MY alarm for 10 P.M., donned a plastic rain poncho over my Valentine surprise, hopped in my car, and drove to WBZE, timing my arrival for a little after ten-thirty, when Michael and I still had an hour or so left to celebrate Valentine's Day in a way he'd never forget.

When I parked in the WBZE lot, I saw that the blinds were lowered in the studio, covering the plate glass window. Perfect. No prying eyes.

I quietly unlocked the front door and crept through the reception area. I heard the sound of running water in the john, so I slipped into the studio and arranged myself in the swivel chair in front of the console. I slid down in the chair, rotating it so the back was facing the studio doorway. When I heard footsteps approaching, I said in my most seductive voice, "Hey, big boy. Happy Valentine's Day. You wanna peel a tomato?" Then, with a big smile on my face, I slowly turned the chair around.

Rick's mouth dropped open to his knees and his face turned as red as my edible underwear.

"Jesus Christ, Rick. What in the hell are you doing here? You were supposed to be off the air at ten." I jumped out of the chair and grabbed my rain poncho. "Where's Michael?"

"He m-m-missed the l-l-last f-f-flight b-b-back from P-p-puerto Rico." Rick was so flustered he was stammering. "He asked me to fill in for him."

"On a school night? What in God's name was he thinking? What will your parents say? Why didn't you call me? Never mind. I'll take his shift. Where's your car?"

"My car's in the shop. I hitched a ride here after school. Michael said it would be all right if I worked for him, that it was too late to call you at home because you'd already be asleep."

"It's okay, Rick. You did what you thought was right and you kept us on the air. I'm grateful to you for that. How much airtime is left on the album you're playing?"

Rick glanced at the album jacket. "Forty minutes."

"Give me five to find some clothes and I'll drive you home." I went into my office and grabbed the shorts and top I'd shed the previous Friday when I'd changed clothes for Miss Lucinda's funeral.

On the way to Rick's house I said, "Do me a favor? If Michael asks, you tell him I came down to the station to pick up some paperwork. But no one ever needs to know what I was wearing. Let's keep that between us. Okay? I'm truly sorry if I made you uncomfortable."

"You got it, Kelly. But can I say one thing?"

I looked over at Rick.

"For someone who's as old as my mom, you still look good in a bikini."

I smiled to myself. "Thanks, Rick. If you ever decide to give up broadcasting, you might try public relations. I think you're a natural."

I drove back to the station, humming "Got Along Withoutcha Before I Metcha, Gonna Get Along Withoutcha Now" under my breath.

Michael definitely had some explaining to do.

# Chapter
# 30

BY THE TIME I got off the air at noon Tuesday, I'd been going for thirteen hours straight on less than five hours sleep but I was finally caught up on WBZE paperwork, except for sorting through a pile of junk mail on the front desk. I went directly home, stopping only at the dumpster to drop a bag filled with fifteen dollars' worth of Valentine surprise into the trash.

After hugging Minx and feeding her an extra helping of kitty stew, I turned off the phone, muted the volume on the answering machine, closed the curtains, and lowered the gallery blinds to keep the afternoon sun outside where it belonged, then flopped facedown on my bed.

When I woke, with Minx curled in the crook of my arm busily washing her face, it was one of those "Who am I? Where am I? What day is it?" moments. I fumbled for the bedside battery-operated clock. Ten after twelve. It was dark outside, so it had to be night. I turned on the radio, heard Michael's voice, turned it off again, and went back to sleep.

When I finally got up at my usual four-fifteen wake-up time, my answering machine was full. I scanned the messages and stopped when I heard Benjamin's voice. "Kelly, Dr. Williams's funeral is Wednesday afternoon. Two o'clock at the Lutheran church. He's being cremated in Puerto Rico, so there will be no burial. I'll see you at the funeral."

I pulled the white dress from my closet along with the dreaded shoes I hoped I'd never have to wear again, grabbed a handful of Band-Aids and a pair of pantyhose, then headed back to WBZE.

Michael was in the studio, where I'd expected to find him thirty hours earlier.

"I thought you went to a funeral last week," he said, looking at the clothes in my arms.

"I did. Miss Lucinda's. There's another one this afternoon."

"Who died?"

"Dr. Williams. You remember him? He's the one who saved me a year ago."

"Mama, I'm sorry. How did he die?"

"A accident on the north shore road last weekend. He crashed into a guard rail." I turned to leave the studio. "Don't go anywhere, Michael. You and I have to talk."

I dropped the clothes in my office, then went to the music library. It felt like a Verdi morning to me. I finally found what I was looking for under "G" instead of "V." Good old Emily's filing system. In a funny way I really missed her.

When Verdi's *Requiem* filled the airwaves, I turned to Michael. "Tell me why you didn't show up for work Monday night. And I don't want to hear any crap about missing the last flight. You were in San Juan for three days."

Michael dropped any pretense at banter and gave it to

me straight. "I'm working on a case. I was following a lead."

"Why didn't you tell me this before you left?"

"Because it's not your need to know."

"You could have let me know you wouldn't be back in time to work."

"I called Rick. He said he'd cover for me."

"Michael, Rick is still in school. He can't work his shift and yours and then go to school without any sleep."

"I did it when I was his age. I bet you did, too. Who pulled my shift?"

"I did, but let's not go there. Does Rick know about your other life?"

"Not from me."

"Me either. I haven't told anyone. What are we going to do, Michael? I've got a radio station to run. I need help I can count on."

"Mama, this case is about over. I think I can promise you it won't happen again." Michael yawned. "I'm getting too old for this double life. I'm thinking of quitting."

"The station?"

"And leave show business?" Michael smiled, then became serious again. "I'm talking about the other thing. But I've got to see this through. I've been working on it for over a year. That gone-bush ex-boyfriend of yours was only the tip of the iceberg. We're after someone much bigger this time. Zip your lip, Mama. It's my ass if this thing blows." He yawned again. "I'm going for coffee. You want anything? We'll talk more when I get back." He reached under the console and handed me a heart-shaped box. "Happy Valentine's Day."

I burst out laughing.

"What's so funny?"

"Do I get to keep the box?" I was laughing so hard my stomach hurt.

"I don't get it."

"It was something Jerry said at the round table. You had to be there. Go get your coffee. Shoo." I waved my hand at Michael as he left the studio for McDonald's.

Inside the box wasn't the assortment of chocolates I was expecting, but a small jeweler's box, stamped with the name of the St. Chris store I'd been in the day after Miss Lucinda's death. I opened the gold foil lid. Nestled on a square of cotton was the sapphire and emerald pendant I'd drooled over, affixed to a simple gold snake chain. I put my fist to my mouth as the tears welled in my eyes.

Michael stood in the studio doorway, watching me as he drank his coffee. "You like it, Mama? The clerk said you'd been looking at it for a long time. I was going to give it to you last weekend in San Juan."

I got up to hug Michael. "I love it. Thank you. I had a surprise for you, too. But it's just too silly to tell you about."

"Try me."

I whispered in his ear.

Michael laughed. "Mama, you are a fox. What's the name of that store?"

We sat in the studio having breakfast. A sausage biscuit and coffee for Michael, a McMuffin and Tab for me.

"There's something heavy going down here, Mama. My informants tell me there's a big shipment of drugs due to hit St. Chris. My guess is it's coming in this weekend."

"Jesus, Michael. Not during the royal visit. That's the last thing we need. St. Chris is going to be crawling with media. We'll all look like bloody fools and the Queen will be humiliated. Can't you do something?"

"I wish I could, Mama. But this is our chance to catch someone really big. It's my job."

"Damn. I wish you hadn't told me. No, I don't mean that."

"Zip your lip, Mama. I'm serious. Not a word to anyone. Not even Ben. This isn't penny-ante poker. Someone could get killed. And I don't want it to be me." He picked the pendant out of the box and fastened the chain around my neck, then stood back to look. "You have good taste, Mama."

I hugged Michael and held him close. "Watch your butt, Michael. I'm very fond of it."

Michael grinned. "What was the name of that store again? I think I've got some more shopping to do."

# Chapter
## 31

THE SMALL WHITE plastered Lutheran church in the center of Isabeya—built in 1769 by the Danes, one of the first buildings completed after the town fire—was filled with mourners for Dr. Williams, many of whom had also attended Miss Lucinda's funeral.

I sat in a cushionless mahogany pew toward the back of the church, slowly fanning my face with the funeral program. The photo of Dr. Williams on the program's cover flitted before my eyes like a drawing in one of those little flip books, predecessors to animated cartoons, where a cat chases a mouse from one side of the page to the other.

I didn't want to think about my conversation with Michael, but it was like trying not to think about an elephant. It was just there. And the royal visit was only three days away. I snapped to attention as the organist played the prelude for the last hymn, and turned to the last page of the program to follow along.

By three-thirty the mourners were filing from the

church, heading down the outside steps to stand in small clusters talking quietly. I felt a hand on my elbow and looked up to see Benjamin and Camille.

"A sad day, Kelly," said Camille. "Dr. Williams delivered Trevor." She pressed her handkerchief to her eyes. "I don't know what this island will do without him."

Benjamin slipped his arm around his wife's waist. "Weren't you going to go pick up Trevor after school today?"

Camille nodded and looked at her watch. "I'd better go. Kelly, would you like to stop by the house for a cold drink on your way home?"

"Thank you, I'd like that."

"Good. I'll see you there." Camille hurried down Kongens Gade toward her car.

"Kelly, let's go for a walk," said Benjamin, guiding me through groups of mourners. "I need to talk to you privately."

"I'm not going anywhere in these shoes, Benjamin." Pantyhose and a triple-thick layer of Band-Aids weren't enough to keep new blisters at bay.

"What is it with women and shoes? Camille spends a fortune on dress-up shoes, but always complains that her feet hurt the minute she puts them on." He looked at my pain-filled face. "Come on. Let's go to the house. I want to get out of this suit and tie."

"Touché, Benjamin," I muttered as I limped along the cross street named Dronningens Tver Gade, looking for my car.

We sat on Benjamin's gallery, drinking iced tea. Benjamin had changed into jeans and a T-shirt. I had shed my shoes, and driven in my stocking feet. My pantyhose and dress felt like Saran Wrap molded to my body.

"Kelly, we haven't got much time. Camille and Trevor will be home any minute. I went to Dr. Williams's office and photocopied his medical examiner file on Miss Lucinda. See what you can make of this." He thrust a sheaf of papers in my hand.

Ancient Egyptian hieroglyphs were easier to decipher than Dr. Williams's handwriting.

"Benjamin, not only do I need a decoder ring, but a medical dictionary would be a big help. I haven't any idea what half of this stuff means."

"Come on, we're going to the hospital."

"In these clothes? Can I change first?"

"Go inside. But hurry."

I went to my car for the clothes I'd worn to work, and changed into my shorts, shirt, and sandals. Benjamin scribbled a note for Camille, and we headed for the St. Chris hospital.

Dr. Williams's office looked like Hurricane Gilda had swept through only moments before we entered.

"Benjamin, is this place always such a mess?"

Benjamin smiled. "Dr. Williams was casual about his filing system. He said he knew where everything was and wouldn't let anyone touch anything. He didn't believe in secretaries. Typed his letters on that old relic." He pointed to a manual typewriter. "You know what he was like. His suits always looked like he slept in them. He was equally casual about taking care of his car. I don't know when he last had a tune-up. You can't run a car without any oil or brake fluid."

I was busy scanning the bookshelves for a medical dictionary, and turned only when I heard the sound of a hand making contact with flesh.

"Benjamin, what's wrong?"

"I'm losing it, Kelly. I need a brain transplant or a vacation. All I've been thinking about lately is the royal visit. Come on. I'm taking you back to the house for your car. I've got work to do."

"Would it be all right if I borrowed these?" I pointed to two volumes on the bookshelf.

"Sure. I'll be responsible for them." Benjamin was standing impatiently at the office door. "Let's get out of here."

I grabbed the books and we left the hospital.

# Chapter
# 32

BENJAMIN DROPPED ME at his house, then U-turned to head back down the driveway.

Camille ran out onto the gallery. "Where is he going in such a hurry?"

"The police station. He said he had some work to do. He'll call you later."

Camille smiled. "This won't be the first time Ben's missed a meal with the family."

Trevor appeared at Camille's side. "Hi, Miss Kelly. Are you staying for dinner? Mom made spaghetti. It's my favorite."

"Please stay, Kelly," said Camille. "There's plenty. We'd love to have you."

I stashed the books in my car then walked in the house, joining Camille and Trevor in the spacious airy kitchen. "What can I do to help you, Camille?"

"Trevor, go wash your hands. Then you can set the table," said Camille.

Trevor marched from the room singing "Heigh-Ho."

Camille smiled as she dumped pasta in a kettle of boiling water. "He's been singing that song all week. I think he's worn out the video."

"We're having a play at school," said Trevor, flashing his still-damp hands in front of Camille before pulling a stack of plates from the cupboard. "I'm going to be the prince. I get to wear a gold crown and a cape. You could come and see me, Miss Kelly."

"I wouldn't miss it, Trevor," I said. "I'll come to your opening night."

"It won't be at night. It's going to be in the afternoon." He paused to take silverware from a drawer, counting each piece. "Did they have plays when you were in school?"

"Forks go on the left, Trevor," said Camille, sliding a pan of garlic bread into the oven. "Kelly, there's a pitcher of iced tea in the refrigerator. Please help yourself. Glasses are in the cupboard. I'll have tea, too."

"Me, too, Mom?"

"No, Trevor. You can have milk with dinner. You're a growing boy."

"Aw, Mom. You always say that."

"Because it's true." Camille pulled Trevor into her arms for a hug and bent down to plant a kiss on the top of his head. "Why don't you go outside and play until dinner's ready? Ten minutes."

"If I go outside, you'll make me wash my hands again before dinner. I'm going to my room to watch television."

A few seconds later we heard the audio track of the *Snow White* video. "Turn that down, Trevor. It's loud enough to wake the dead." Camille picked up her glass of iced tea. "Kids," she said, shaking her head. "Why does everything have to be played at full blast?" I followed her onto the gallery. "I spend half my time at school saying, 'Turn that down.' We finally had to ban boom boxes completely." She sat and stretched her legs. "Peace. It's wonderful."

We watched the shadows lengthen and listened to the palm fronds swish like exotic fringed fans in the evening breeze. "Have you decided what to wear to the garden party, Kelly? It'll be long dresses, of course, for the royal dinner. Ben is already complaining about having to put on his dinner jacket. Trevor wanted a tux of his own for the garden party, but I put my foot down. It's totally inappropriate. He can wear the navy blue suit we bought him last Christmas."

A timer bell dinged in the kitchen, saving me from either telling a bald-faced lie or else having to admit I hadn't been invited to the garden party. Camille rose from her chair. "Kelly, will you get Trevor out of his room while I put the food on the table?"

Trevor's bedroom door was open, so I walked in without knocking to find him sitting on the floor watching his video. His room was filled with all the things eight-year-old boys seem to love: baseball bat and glove, models hung from the ceiling, books scattered on the floor, a computer on his desk. On the whole, his room was a lot neater than Dr. Williams's office.

"Watch this, Miss Kelly. Snow White is singing to the dwarfs about the prince."

"Trevor! Now!" called Camille.

He reluctantly turned off the video. "We can see the rest after dinner. It gets real scary later."

After a delicious dinner of spaghetti and garlic bread, I helped Camille clean up the kitchen while Trevor did his homework. Then I headed for home to feed Minx and spend the evening translating Dr. Williams's notes with the help of the books I'd borrowed.

While Minx was chowing down her dinner of liver and chicken mixed with cat crunchies, I went to brush my teeth to get the lingering taste of garlic bread out of my mouth. That's when the lightbulb I call my little voice went off in my head like a megawatt strobe. I spit the mouthwash into the sink and ran to my desk. There, scribbled in a handwriting that only a pharmacist could easily decode, were words: *garlic—flu?* Following that was one word: *disulfiram?*

What in the hell was disulfiram?

I sank to the floor and pulled the *Physicians' Desk Reference*—a ten-pound tome I'd borrowed from Dr. Williams's office—into my lap and I thumbed through the pages until I found the index.

After scanning the entry I was looking for, I thrust the book from my lap. It landed with a plop on my terrazzo floor that made Minx jump and hiss.

I grabbed the phone and speed-dialed Benjamin's number. Camille answered. "Camille, I wanted to thank you again for a really great dinner. Please have Benjamin call me when he's got a minute."

If my hunch was right, then what had looked like Miss Lucinda's bout of the flu was really the reaction of disulfiram mixed with gin.

I crawled into bed to finish rereading Agatha Christie's *Mysterious Affair at Styles.* When I turned off the light at nine, I thought to myself that strychnine was a hell of a way to die, but that Christie had handled it very cleverly and her book could serve as a classic text on murder.

# Chapter

# 33

I HATE IT when I wake up with a tune running through my head that I can't shake. It's like that not thinking about elephants thing. The more I try not to hear the song, the more insistent it is. Like a sore tooth demanding attention.

When I reached the station, I was still humming that damned song from Trevor's video. Benjamin groaned when he heard me singing as I got out of my car.

"You too? I told Camille to bury that video in the back-yard when Trevor went to school. He plays it day and night. It's driving me nuts."

"He's getting into his part for the play. Actors do that."

"How would you know? I forgot. Camille and I have seen you in shows at the community theater. You're very good for an amateur."

I bit my tongue to hide the smile playing on my lips, while mentally kicking myself for saying anything about acting. One of these days my big mouth was going to get me in trouble, if I inadvertently spilled the beans about my professional acting past and the six months I'd spent in the original Chicago company of *Hair*. "What are you doing here so early? Did you come to make a request for the morning classics?"

"Camille said you wanted to talk to me. I didn't get home until almost ten last night and today's going to be a long one. I spent the evening with a mechanic going over Dr. Williams's car."

"What did you find out?"

"I think his brakes were tampered with before the accident."

"Damn. Are you sure?"

"There was no brake fluid left. It looked like the lines might have been snipped to create a slow leak. I told you before Dr. Williams always drove too fast. When he hit the curve on the north shore road, he couldn't slow down. Only the guardrail kept him from flying off the road into the sea."

"But if the guardrail had given way, he might have survived," I said. "I've owned several VW Beetles and they float like Ivory soap."

"Now I've got a new case on my hands," said Benjamin with a sigh. "But there's nothing I can do about it until after the royal visit." He rubbed his eyes and shook his head to force himself awake. "What did you want to talk to me about?"

"It's complicated. Come and sit down for a minute while I tell you."

Benjamin and I sat on the stoop in front of the WBZE entrance. Behind us the sky was slowly brightening. In front of us the autosensor street lamps dimmed, then died.

"Do you remember the champagne toast the night of Miss Maude's dinner?" I asked.

"Sure. Chris made a speech thanking Miss Maude and we all drank. What about it?"

"There was one person that night who raised a glass, but didn't drink."

Benjamin turned to stare at me. "Who was that?"

"Miss Lucinda."

"Son of a bitch."

"She raised the glass to her lips, but then I heard her mumble under her breath, 'Champagne makes me windy,' and she put the glass down untasted."

"You're absolutely right. I'd forgotten all about it."

"We all got sick that night, remember?"

"That I'll never forget. I don't think I've ever been so sick in my life. Not even when I had dengue fever last fall."

"And we all thought it was fish poisoning, but it turned out not to be true."

"Kelly, get to the point."

"Humor me, Benjamin. One more question: When you were sick, did you taste garlic?"

"God, yes. I complained to Camille about it and she said she tasted the same thing."

"Miss Maude said she didn't cook with garlic that evening because of Miss Lucinda's ulcer."

"Will you cut to the chase?"

I went to my car and came back with a book. I opened it to the page I'd marked. "Listen to this. A metallic or garlic-like aftertaste may be experienced during the first two weeks of therapy.' "

"Therapy? What therapy?"

"Disulfiram. Also known as Antabuse. A drug often prescribed for alcoholics to curb their drinking."

"Wait a minute," said Benjamin. "I'm not making the connection."

"Try this on for size. The champagne was laced with disulfiram, making us all sick. After all, that's the point of it. You mix Antabuse with booze, you get sick. But because we'd already eaten a heavy meal—remember, everyone had second helpings that night—and the disulfiram was mixed with a low-proof wine, we didn't feel the effects right away. When we did get sick, we all thought it was fish poisoning. The symptoms are very similar."

"But it wasn't fish poisoning. We proved that after I found Miss Maude's trash at the dump."

"Exactly. So we blamed getting sick on the flu, which was the next logical conclusion. The flu's been going around St. Chris since Christmas like a brush fire."

"So who was responsible?"

I ticked three points off on my fingers as I spoke. "There was one person who had the means, the disulfiram; the opportunity, everyone was in and out of Miss Maude's kitchen that night; and the motive."

"I'm with you on means and opportunity. What's the motive?"

"Jealousy. The green-eyed monster."

"Kelly, you can't be serious. You've been reading too many mysteries. You need to get a life."

I looked at Benjamin over the top of my sunglasses. "You think so? You told me yourself there was someone who couldn't stand being ignored or upstaged. Who's been getting all the attention in connection with the royal visit?"

"Miss Maude."

"And who was her best friend?"

"Miss Lucinda?"

I nodded emphatically, losing my sunglasses in the process. "I rest my case." I bent down to pick up my glasses.

Benjamin leaned back and laced his fingers behind his head. I could see the wheels turning and kept as quiet as a lizard while he thought about what I'd said.

The silence was interrupted by Michael opening the front door. "Mama, I've got you covered."

I looked at my watch. Six-oh-five. "Benjamin, come inside with me. I've got to get on the air."

"Chill, Mama. You're gold until seven. I segued from my show right into yours. I put on the Bernstein-Gershwin album. The one that runs a few seconds over an hour and opens with "Symphonic Dances" from *West Side Story*. Right about now"—Michael paused to look at his watch— 'Somewhere' is kicking off. I'm going for coffee. You want some, Ben? Mama, you want a McMuffin?"

While Michael went for food and coffee, Benjamin and I moved into the studio to continue our conversation.

"Miss Lucy? Who would ever have suspected her?" said Benjamin. "There's no crime in making someone sick, but it was a very wicked thing for Miss Lucy to do. Miss Maude was so devastated she wanted to cancel the royal dinner completely."

"Exactly what Miss Lucinda intended."

"And all because of jealousy. Jesus." Benjamin slowly exhaled and shook his head sadly.

Michael walked into the studio carrying a large brown McDonald's bag. "Chow down, guys. Ben, I brought an extra McMuffin for you. If you don't want it, give it to Mama." He leaned down to kiss me, then headed for the door. "Gotta grab some z's. Catch you later. Where are you gonna be tonight, Mama?"

"Fairground. Working on the homestead house."

Michael saluted smartly and split.

Benjamin grabbed the McMuffin. "Don't tell Camille. She refers to fast food as heart attacks to go."

When we had finished eating, I said, "There's more. But I don't think you're going to like what I have to say."

"I'm a step ahead of you. You going to tell me Miss Maude killed Miss Lucy. And I'm going to tell you you're crazy." Benjamin pounded the console with his fist, sloshing coffee onto the log sheet.

I grabbed a napkin and began mopping. "But don't you see, Benjamin? The same reasons apply. Miss Maude also had means, opportunity, and motive. I think she gave Miss Lucinda a taste of her own medicine in order to save the royal visit. It means so much to Miss Maude to have Queen Margrethe and Prince Henrik here."

"I knew this damned royal visit was going to be big trouble," said Benjamin. "But everyone kept saying how good it would be for St. Chris, so I kept my concerns to myself." He sighed deeply. "I can't arrest Miss Maude on suspicion of murder. She was my schoolteacher. She taught me how to read and write. I've known her all my life. I'll have to get someone else to arrest her. But not until after the royal visit. Camille and Amelia would never forgive me. And if our suspicions are wrong, I'd never forgive myself."

Benjamin looked at me with an intensity that scared the devil out of me. "Promise me, Kelly, that everything we said this morning stays between us. Not a single word to anyone. Not even Michael. I want you to smile the whole damned weekend. Even if it kills you. Can you do that?"

I promised I would. Even if it nearly cost me my life.

Benjamin stormed out of WBZE without saying goodbye.

# Chapter
# 34

I SPENT THE morning thinking of all the things I'd said to Benjamin, and those I had not. It bothered me that someone I considered a friend was now angry with me, but it bothered me even more that someone I held in high regard had resorted to murder to achieve her own ends.

When I had lived in Chicago, murder was a fact of life. It was even celebrated, in a macabre sort of way, in the legends surrounding John Dillinger and Al Capone. Mention the Biograph Theater where Dillinger was captured and the words "lady in red" come to mind. I had once fingered the bullet holes in the wall of the garage on Chicago's north side that was the scene of the Saint Valentine's Day Massacre. A wall that was eventually sold and was now part of someone's rec room. When Richard Speck murdered the student nurses a few blocks away from an apartment I later rented, every single woman in Chicago was scared out of her wits. But one expects crime in a city of six million faceless strangers. One doesn't expect it on a small tropical island where everyone knows everyone else.

My promise to Benjamin was put to its first test when the phone rang at nine-thirty. When I heard the voice on the other end of the line, I kicked myself for not having gotten around to hiring a receptionist.

"Good morning, Miss Maude," I said with as much cheer as I could muster, being careful not to overdo it.

"Kelly, dear, I know how busy we all are with the royal visit only two days away, but I wonder if you could do me a small favor?"

"Sure. What is it?"

"Would you meet me at the bank next Tuesday? The rent is coming due on Lucy's safe-deposit box so I thought I'd close it out and put the contents in my own box. I'd feel more comfortable if someone else was there with me."

I was racked by a sudden coughing fit and reached for my Tab.

"Kelly? Are you all right? You really should do something about that cough. What you need is bush tea."

Miss Maude rang off and I sat back in my chair to think.

I hadn't told Benjamin about Miss Lucinda's trust, or that Miss Maude was the sole surviving trustee and the inheritor of Miss Lucinda's personal effects and jewelry, which in itself was a motive for murder. Was it really legal for someone to benefit from a crime they'd committed? I picked up the phone to call out, but put down the receiver before I'd pushed the first digit. Benjamin had made it very clear he'd had enough of me for one morning.

Margo called at eleven. "Kel, have you been hibernating? I haven't seen you since Monday. Get your butt to the Watering Hole for lunch. You'll never guess what happened. Hang on for a sec, will you?" I heard muffled sounds as if Margo had put her hand over the phone. "Sorry about that, Kel. I've got to go, a hot prospect just walked in the door. See you in an hour."

Traffic at noon on Kongens Gade was even worse than at five o'clock. A cruise ship had made an unscheduled stop to give its passengers a taste of the upcoming royal visit. I sat impatiently in my car, behind a caravan of creeping taxi vans, watching the needle on my temperature gauge move steadily upward from C to H. Just when I thought my temper would explode along with my overheated car, we surged forward. I grabbed the first legal parking space I found, one that was so far from the Watering Hole I might as well have been parking back in the WBZE lot, and hoofed it through the crowds. By the time I got to the round table, sweat was dripping off my ears and I was in a thoroughly grumpy mood.

"Where is everyone?" I said to Abby. "Margo called me this morning and told me to get my butt here for lunch. She said there was a surprise."

"Look behind you, Kel," said Abby, pointing in the air to a spot somewhere behind my left shoulder.

I turned to stare at the Watering Hole chalkboard.

"So?"

"Read what's on it."

"Special today: *Bikesmad Med Spejlaeg* (fried potatoes with diced meat and a fried egg) or *Braendende Kaerlighed* (mashed potatoes with bacon and onions)." I groaned. "Danish mania strikes again. I thought we were all through with that. What happened to the veggie burgers?"

"You don't get it, Kel. The old chef is back!"

"Be still, my arteries. When did that happen?"

"This morning. I spent the past three days with Immigration getting his green card status straightened out. You guys owe me forever."

"Abby, I'm so grateful I'll buy your lunch today."

"Oh damn. Abby, you spoiled the surprise," Margo said as she pulled out her chair.

"It's your fault for being a slowpoke," said Abby.

"I think we ought to be singing 'Happy Days Are Here Again,' " I said. "I was about to give up eating in town forever."

"You and me both," said Margo.

"What'll it be, ladies?" said Carole, pulling her order pad out of her pocket.

"Medium-rare burgers with all the trimmings and extra fries," we said in unison.

"How about a Danish Mary on the house to start?"

"Carole!"

"Okay, okay. It was just a suggestion. The cruise ship passengers are really going for it. We're finally running out of aquavit. Iced tea and iced coffee, right? You got it."

"Kel, can you stand it?" said Margo. "Two days and we'll be getting ready to meet the Queen. I'm taking tomorrow afternoon off to have my hair and nails done."

"Really?" I said. "You too, Abby?"

"My manicure appointment isn't until four," said Abby. "I've got to be in court all morning and most of the afternoon."

"Where's Jerry?" I asked.

"I don't know," said Margo. "I haven't seen him all day. He's probably sucking up at Government House. You know how Jerry loves to be in on all the action. I wish he'd spend some time at Island Palms. I could use the help. We're getting busy. The royal visit has been very good for the real estate business. Oh my God. Look over there!"

We turned to see a network camera crew shooting background footage. The royal visit had unofficially begun.

# Chapter
# 35

As I WALKED back to my car, neatly sidestepping the cruise ship passengers filling the narrow Isabeya sidewalks looking at Department of Tourism gift shop maps and taking pictures of each other looking at the maps, I realized that my home larder was decidedly bare; unless I did something about it PDQ, I was going to have one pissed-off pussycat on my hands.

I drove to the supermarket, located in the shopping area west of town that was also home to McDonald's. I'd wheeled my way through produce and bottled juices and was aiming for the cat food section when I ran into Miss Maude and Elodia pushing loaded shopping carts.

"Kelly," said Miss Maude, "what a pleasant surprise."

"I usually shop on Saturday morning," I said. "But with the royal visit, I thought I'd get it done early this week."

"How very wise. By any chance are you going home when you're through shopping?"

I nodded.

"Would you mind dropping Elodia at Lucy's house?

She was kind enough to help me with the shopping for this weekend, but I find I'm running short of time. It would be an enormous favor to me if you'd take her home so I can get these frozen things into my freezer as quickly as possible."

"I'd be glad to, Miss Maude. Elodia, why don't you wait for me inside the front door? I won't be very long and it's too hot for you to stand outside."

By the time I had finished my own shopping—which consisted of cat food, Tab, toilet paper, cheese, chicken, and a couple of steaks—Miss Maude was pulling out of the parking lot in her Land Rover. I breezed through the checkout in far less time than it would have taken on a Saturday morning. Elodia and I piled into my car with our groceries and headed for the south shore.

When we arrived at Miss Lucinda's house, I offered to carry Elodia's groceries inside for her.

"Thank you," she said. "My fingers are stiff today and those heavy plastic bags cut my hands like knives."

I put the bags on the kitchen counter.

"Would you like a cup of tea?" she asked. "Miss Lucy and I always have our tea and biscuits after we do the shopping."

"Tea would be lovely," I said.

"I'll bring it to Miss Lucy's sitting room," said Elodia. "It's just down the hall."

"I remember where it is," I said. I walked into the sitting room and sat on a chintz-covered loveseat until Elodia arrived with the tea tray.

"That's Miss Lucy's favorite spot," Elodia said.

"Did she entertain in this room?"

"Oh no. This is Miss Lucy's private room. She received most of her guests in the library, but she always sit in here when she look at her picture books."

"Picture books? Which books are those?" I asked.

"I'll show you." Elodia crossed to a built-in cupboard and opened it. Inside were a stack of photo albums. She picked one and handed it to me. "Miss Lucy often looked at this one."

I opened the book while Elodia poured our tea from a small china pot. Waiting for her tea to cool, Elodia began humming tunelessly under her breath.

I glanced at page after page of old sepia photographs. Miss Lucinda as a very young girl, Miss Lucinda as a young girl at school and with friends. Toward the back of the album was a debut photo of Miss Lucinda that absolutely took my breath away. Margo was right. In her late teens Miss Lucinda had been a radiant beauty. As I bent over the album to get a closer look at the portrait, the phone rang. Elodia scurried off to the kitchen to answer it. Old habits die hard, I thought.

I lifted the portrait out of the corner mounts. Fixed to the back with yellowed, brittle cellophane tape was a smaller black and white photograph. The type taken with an old box camera. There was no mistaking Miss Lucinda, the watch on her left wrist, or the boyish smile of the man dressed in a kilt and sporran standing next to her with his arm around her waist. I'd seen enough old newsreels and read enough biographies to know that smile could only belong to the former Prince of Wales.

# Chapter
# 36

THE FAIRGROUND WAS buzzing like a nest of Jack Spaniards plotting an ambush on a hapless tourist.

Under mercury vapor lights positioned throughout the fairground like giant beanstalks reaching for the sky, the midway rides were being set up. The merry-go-round and bumper cars were already in place and the Ferris wheel was being erected.

"Trevor, you come away from there! You could get hurt. I need you here," yelled Camille, who was busy supervising the unloading of a truck filled with old furniture.

The building crew was doing a final touch-up to our exterior paint job.

Maubi's van pulled up alongside the homestead house. "Morning Lady, come see what I got this afternoon."

I put down my paintbrush and walked over to the van.

Through the passenger door a familiar male voice called out, "Remember me, Kelly?"

"Quincy! Welcome home! Maubi said you were coming back for spring break."

Quincy jumped out of the van. Trevor ran up and threw himself in Quincy's arms. "Trevor, my main man. Look at you. You're growing faster than tan-tan." Trevor grinned.

"Quincy, you look great," I said. "How's college?"

"It's good, but it's a lot tougher than I thought it would be."

"Don't let him fool you, Morning Lady," said Maubi, beaming at his son. "Quincy got A's on his report card."

"I'm glad to be home," said Quincy. "It's cold up there in Ithaca. I'm not used to the cold. I miss my family, my friends, our warm weather and trade winds."

"Be glad you weren't here for the hurricane. That was more wind than any of us ever wanted to see."

"You make out okay? How's Michael?"

"I'm good. Michael's good. He'll be around this weekend and I know he wants to see you. You come see me at the radio station while you're home. We'll talk about a summer job."

"Thanks, Kelly. I heard Harborview went bush in the storm."

"It's being rebuilt, but won't be open until next season."

"Quincy, come on. Let's go look at the rides," said Trevor, tugging on Quincy's arm. "As soon as it's ready, I want to go on the Ferris wheel. I asked Miss Kelly to ride with me, but she said she doesn't like heights." Quincy laughed and took off with Trevor.

I went back to my painting. Camille continued unloading the truck. There was no sign of either Benjamin or Miss Maude.

Amelia drove up in her minivan. She opened the side door and began hauling out bundles of curtains. "Granny

Maude is home making red grout tonight while the art students are finishing the murals on her fence. Benjamin's over there limin' on the gallery like good old Tom Sawyer. He calls that supervising. Granny Maude sent me with the curtains. I hope someone remembered to get curtain rods."

"My grandmama Alveena never have curtain rods," said Maubi. "She use wire or skinny rope. I got some in my van."

While Maubi nailed twine over the inside window frames, Amelia hung the curtains Miss Maude had made from the flowered fabric belonging to her own mother. The homestead house was beginning to look like a real home.

"The Ferris wheel's not ready yet," said Trevor. "How long does it take?"

Quincy was put to work with a broom sweeping the inside of the house before the braided throw rugs and simple wooden furniture were put in place. Trevor followed behind Quincy with a dust pan.

"Trevor, don't dump the dirt on the ground. Put it in the trash barrel," said Camille.

We stashed the paint cans, the brushes, and the broom in the outhouse before decorating the main house.

"Amelia, did you remember the kitchen stuff?" said Camille.

"No. I was in such a hurry to get to Granny Maude's to pick up the curtains, I forgot all about it. It's in two boxes next to my back door. I'll bring it tomorrow night."

"I got some old things that belong to Alveena," said Maubi. "Quincy, get that box out of the van."

Trevor ran up to Camille, panting. "Mom, the Ferris wheel is up now and the man said I can ride for free. Is it okay?"

"Only if you go with an adult, Trevor. I'm busy now."

"Come on, Miss Kelly. It's not real high. Please?"

Quincy turned to Camille. "I'll take Trevor, if it's all right with you."

"Okay, Trevor. You can go with Quincy. But just one ride. It's a school night and we have to get home. You have all weekend to go on the Ferris wheel."

By the time Quincy and Trevor got back from riding the Ferris wheel—"It's really super, Mom. You can see the whole fairground from up there. I bet during the day you can see all the way to the west end of the island."— we'd finished furnishing and decorating the homestead house. We lit the kerosene lanterns just to see the effect.

As Maubi stood looking at the house, tears welled in his eyes. "If only my grandparents were here to see this."

Quincy walked up behind Maubi and put his arms around him, his chin grazing Maubi's ear. They stood, father and son, gazing silently at the small wooden house. I felt a lump in my own throat, and then Camille's slim cool hand squeezing mine.

A Government House car sped through the fairground entrance, pausing first at the midway, then stopping next to Maubi's van. A tinted window silently opened and Chris called out, "Looking good. I'll be back tomorrow night for the final inspection. You've all done a great job. The governor will be very pleased." The car exited the fairground, turning left onto the main road leading to Isabeya.

"If he be so damn pleased, why don't he say so with his own face," muttered Maubi, turning away from the house to cross to his van. He picked up an ice cream scoop and called through the serving window, "I got homemade ice cream for everybody."

Trevor was first in line as we all stampeded for the serving window.

# Chapter
# 37

"MAMA, ARE YOU ready for the big doings this weekend?"

Those were the first words out of Michael's mouth when I walked into the studio Friday morning, a little more than twenty-four hours before Queen Margrethe was due to arrive on St. Chris.

"As ready as I'll ever be," I said, looking at my hands, which were still paint-splattered and badly needed a manicure.

"I know we're due at Miss Maude's for dinner tomorrow night at seven. That's black tie, right?"

"Right."

"And the garden party is in the afternoon at Government House. What's the dress code?"

"Michael, I don't know how to break this to you. I wasn't invited to the garden party."

"Of course you were. But if you don't want to go, that's cool."

"Read my lips. I wasn't invited."

"I saw the invitation. Chill, Mama. I'll get it."

Michael went into the reception area and returned a few minutes later with an unopened buff envelope in his hand.

"Where was this?" I asked.

"In a pile of junk mail and magazines on Emily's desk. I saw it early this morning when I was looking for something to read. It must have been delivered in a batch of mail when you were off duty."

I used a letter opener to slit the envelope. Inside was a formal engraved invitation to the garden party. Who would have guessed it would be sent to the station rather than my personal address? I felt like an idiot for thinking I hadn't been invited and for caring so much about it. Obsession with royalty was more infectious than the flu.

"Looks like we're on for the garden party," I said.

"Can I go as I am?"

I looked at Michael's baggy shorts, flowered aloha shirt, and flip-flops that were so run down they made mine look almost new. "Sure. And I'll wear a grass skirt and two hibiscus blossoms. We'll be the hit of the party."

"Later, Mama. Gotta pick up my suit and tux at the cleaners, then I'm getting my hair cut at nine. I'll try and catch up with you later. Where are you going to be?"

"I'll be at the fairground after six. Tonight is the final prep for the fair opening. I told Camille I'd help with the school exhibits. Between the school kids and the down-island vendors setting up shop, the exhibit hall is going to be a zoo. And I just know Trevor is going to badger me to ride the damned Ferris wheel with him."

"You on a Ferris wheel? This I gotta see." Michael began singing "Up, Up and Away" at the top of his lungs.

"Put a sock in it, Michael."

When I picked up the clipboard to swat at him like a pesky insect, he ducked and ran for the studio doorway. "Hey, Michael! I forgot to tell you. Quincy's home for spring break. He asked about you last night."

Michael blew me a kiss from the safety of the hall. "Tell Quincy I'll catch up with him this weekend."

I tucked the garden party invitation in my tote so I wouldn't lose it, then sat down to make out the weekly payroll. I gave Rick a small bonus for working overtime, but decided against docking Michael's pay for the night he missed. If I thought about it real hard, I could probably find a way for Michael to make it up to me.

After a morning spent filing my nails and picking the paint off my hands while mentally ransacking my closet for something to wear to the garden party, I ran out of the station the second I was off the air and drove the few short blocks into town to do my banking.

The bank was already closed for the three-day holiday weekend.

"What the hell?" I read the sign posted on the door: WE ARE CLOSING TODAY AT NOON IN HONOR OF THE ROYAL VISIT. As if twenty-three annual holidays weren't enough. I admit it, I was jealous. There were no holidays for deejays. In my next life I wanted a bank job.

The streets and sidewalks were busier than Christmas Eve, thronged with gleeful government workers departing their offices for the unexpected halfday holiday. I put my deposit in the night slot, then joined the line at the ATM to get some ready cash.

"Grab a couple of fifties for me," a voice said behind me.

"Hey, Jerry. What's up? You look like one of the lost boys from *Peter Pan*."

"I got booted out of my office. Government House is shut down tight to get ready for tomorrow. It's a security thing. Let's go have a drink at the Watering Hole. I'll buy."

I put my hand on Jerry's forehead. "You're not running a fever. Are you sure you're feeling all right?"

"Very funny, Kel."

"I take it back, Jerry. You're really Grumpy from *Snow White*."

"Bag the short jokes. You want a drink or not?"

I looked at my watch. "I've got time for a quick one. Then I've got to get home."

We locked arms and skipped down the sidewalk singing "We're Off to See the Wizard" to the amusement of one and all. When we arrived at the Watering Hole, we stopped dead in our tracks.

The round table was filled with tourists.

"Guys, I'm really sorry," said Carole. "I didn't think you'd show up today. This place has been a madhouse all morning. The media, tourists. Can you imagine what it's going to be like tomorrow?" She glanced at the bar. "If you'll sit at the bar—just this once, please? I promise it'll never happen again—your drinks and lunch are on the house."

Jerry purred.

"Nice going, Jerry," I said with a smile. "You lucked out again."

"Kel, I said I would buy you a drink. I didn't say I was going to pay for it."

I jabbed him with my elbow as we took our seats at the bar.

While we sipped our drinks and ate Danish club sandwiches—the Friday special: Danish ham, Danish bacon, with lettuce and tomato, on Danish rye—conversation about the royal visit swirled around us.

"What time is the Queen arriving?"

"I heard she's going to walk around town. Where's the best place to see her?"

"Would she be upset if I asked for her autograph?"

"The *Danmark* is coming tomorrow. Those Danish sailors are so cute."

Jerry pointed his index finger at his mouth and made a gagging sound. "Can't people talk about anything but the royal visit?"

I patted his arm. "It's like Christmas. You spend a month getting ready for it, and before you have time to kick back and enjoy it, it's all over. Next week the royal visit will be history. Then what will we talk about? The weather?" I took another bite of my sandwich. "This is delicious. The chef finally got it right. Say, Jerry. What was that wine you served with your lasagna? Margo said it was really good. I'd love to get a bottle. Where did you find it?"

Jerry's mouth was too full to talk.

"Come on, Jerry. You can tell me. I only want one bottle. If you've got a secret source, I promise I won't tell Margo."

Jerry swallowed, glanced over his shoulder, then leaned close to me and whispered in my ear, "I liberated it."

"You what?"

"I liberated it from Government House."

"Jesus, Jerry. What were you doing in the governor's wine cellar?"

"He'll never miss it. No one's seen the governor for weeks, but what else is new? Besides, it wasn't in the wine cellar."

"Where was it?"

"In Chris's office. He had a bunch of open bottles in there. I think they were samples for the royal lunch. I know he didn't pay for them. What's the harm? He was going to dump it out anyway. Wine goes bad once it's uncorked. Don't tell Margo. She'll never let me hear the end of it. She loves telling me how cheap I am."

"My lips are sealed, sweetie." I mimed zipping my lips and throwing away the key.

"There you are!"

We turned to find Victoria standing behind us, looking exceedingly frazzled.

"Jerry, what on earth is going on at Government House? I've been trying to reach Chris on the phone all morning long and no one answers. I just came from there and it's locked tighter than the crown jewels in the Tower of London."

"Everyone was given the day off to get ready for the royal visit," said Jerry. "I haven't seen Chris since yesterday. Security booted me out of my office early this morning."

"Oh, for Lord's sake. You'd think there would be at least one person around to answer the blasted phone. How am I supposed to get everything done for the lunch and garden party? I can't get through the Government House gate without a special pass. And Chris has the passes. If you see him, tell him to call me!"

We heard her exclaim as she flew out of sight, "I'm going to get in there if I have to scale the ruddy fence!"

# Chapter
## 38

I WENT HOME to polish my nails with Hot Gooey Stuff—a shade made for the bubblegum crowd that's barely pink with a hint of frost which still looks presentable if chipped—and root through my closet like a pig in a forest nosing for truffles.

Two hours—and a bed full of discarded garments—later, I finally struck pay dirt.

For me, there's only one color for dress-up occasions and that's black. I look like hell in pippy-poo pastels and Laura Ashley–type floral prints; and I abhor anything with ruffles or bows. They make me feel like Shirley Temple playing Heidi.

For the garden party, a sleeveless cotton piqué with a jewel neck and slightly flared skirt, the easier to attempt a curtsy when introduced to Her Majesty. Then for Miss Maude's dinner, a formal-length silk with an empire waist and tiny spaghetti straps, topped with a black sequined jacket. Both dresses were just right for my new sapphire and emerald pendant.

Back into the closet for shoes and a purse, then to my dresser to check my supply of off-black pantyhose.

One thing the guidebooks never tell you about living on a Caribbean island is the effect of heat, humidity, and salt air on elastic. Until you've experienced having your underwear slide to your knees as you walk down the street, you don't know the meaning of perishable.

My never-worn, still-in-the-package pantyhose were completely shot. Margo said she kept hers in the freezer— they lasted longer.

I had exactly forty-five minutes to get to the chain store for replacements. I heard the phone ring as I ran out of the house, but had no time to talk. Let the machine get it.

There were three pairs of pantyhose left in my size. I bought them all. I tossed the package in the back seat of my car and zigzagged through the maze of parked cars to get to the road leading to the fairground.

If I thought the shopping center was jammed, it was a wasteland compared to the fairground. I hadn't seen so many people and vehicles in one place since the Easter weekend camp-out at Columbus Bay.

An Ag Fair worker was standing in the basket of a cherry picker at one side of the fairground entrance, hanging a canvas banner across the entrance that read:

*Back to Our Roots*
*Velkommen Queen Margrethe og Prince Henrik*

On the left of the banner was the Danish flag, the red and white Dannebrog; and on the right the St. Chris flag, with its bright tropical colors of blue, green, white, and yellow.

A guard stopped me from driving into the parking lot. "You unloading?"

I shook my head.

"Park along the road."

I drove along the side road until I came to an empty spot and backed into the edge of a field, hoping I wasn't driving over cassia, a plant laden with thorns that loves to eat tires. The last thing I needed was a flat.

As I locked my car, the sun was setting in a cloudless sky chased by Mercury, Saturn, and Venus. A half-moon shone directly overhead. The weekend forecast was the weather tourists pray for when they book their winter vacations: clear skies, highs upper eighties to low nineties, lows lower seventies, easterly winds ten to twenty miles an hour, chance of rain twenty percent. The twenty percent was a fudge factor. We hadn't had rain in weeks.

The first person I saw that I knew was Amelia.

"Kelly, am I glad to see you. Grab one of these boxes, will you? It's the kitchen stuff for the homestead house."

I hoisted a box that had once been filled with reams of copy machine paper and we wriggled our way through the crowds to the shuttered and locked homestead house.

"We'll put these in the kitchen. Camille and Maubi can finish arranging everything later. I've got to get back to Granny Maude's. The way she's cooking, you'd think she was feeding an army instead of only twelve. I don't know how she does it. I would have had the dinner catered."

Amelia waved goodbye and ran back to her minivan.

I peeked in the food hall, where the church ladies were setting up their tables and posting their menus before going home to finish preparing the food that would be on sale after the Queen cut the ribbon officially opening the fair.

In the outside wooden booths, the independent food vendors were busy testing electrical outlets and running extension cords to glass cases fitted with infrared lamps. Strings of miniature Danish flags, fluttering softly in the dying breeze, were affixed to every stationary object.

I crossed the little bridge over the gut running through the fairground and walked along the midway, past more wooden booths where souvenir sellers were stocking their shelves with everything from T-shirts to pinwheels and noisemakers to bead jewelry and glow-stick necklaces.

A vendor waved a neon-colored noodle. "Prefair special. Your choice of colors. Only a dollar. Tomorrow the price goes up."

I dug in my fanny pack for a dollar bill. I snapped the jade green tube, which began immediately glowing like the phosphorescent sea, hooked the ends together, and slipped it over my head, to hang around my neck.

I continued past the fenced pens where award-contending goats, sheep, pigs, and cattle were being reluctantly quartered in their temporary homes. Eau de goat reminded me of how my house had reeked when I first bought it. A stench finally eradicated by gallons of Lysol, but one that crept back into the air when the humidity topped ninety.

At last I reached the exhibit hall, which resembled a cross between London's Covent Garden in the days when Eliza Doolittle held court, and Chicago's McCormick Place when a trade show was in town.

The large rectangular building ran north to south, with huge double doors on the east and west sides of the southern end.

The spaces for plant vendors were on the southern end of the building, closest to the doors, for ease in unloading flats of seedlings, bags of fertilizer, and large potted plants, palms, and fruit trees. I saw some of the plant sellers standing next to their loaded trucks and vans, impatiently checking their watches. They would unload last, after the school exhibits were set up at the far end of the building.

I finally found Camille at the high school exhibit area. "Amelia wanted mė to tell you the kitchen stuff is here. I helped her carry it to the homestead house. She said you and Maubi would arrange it later."

Camille wiped her brow with the back of her hand. "What time is it?"

I glanced at my watch. "Seven-twenty."

"I'll meet you at the homestead house at eight-thirty. We've got to be out of the exhibit hall by eight on the dot so the down-island vendors and plant sellers can get in to set up." She looked around the booth. "What do you think?"

I looked at a scale model of an 1820 sugar plantation. Tiny carts pulled by mules were hauling bundles of cut cane to the thimble-shaped mill for processing. In the fields workers were cutting more cane. Stalks of real sugar cane had been placed around the sides of the booth.

"It's wonderful. The detail is exquisite. Look, there's even a little dinner bell hanging in the tamarind tree. Your students did a great job. It should be in a museum."

"Trevor, there you are!" said Camille. "Where have you been? I told you not to go running off."

"I've been helping set up the booth for my school, Mom. But we're all through now. Can I go play? Dad said I could."

"All right, Trevor. But meet me at the homestead house at eight-thirty. Tomorrow's a big day and we need to get home early tonight. Kelly, did Ben find you?"

"No, I haven't seen him. Why?"

"I don't know. He came home late this afternoon to change clothes and said he had to talk to you."

"Miss Kelly, where did you get that cool necklace? I want one. How much was it?"

"Come on, Trevor, I'll buy you one," I said.

"Trevor has his own money, Kelly. He's been saving

for the fair." Camille turned to her son. "Don't spend it all before the fair's even started. And remember: homestead house, eight-thirty."

"Okay, Mom." Trevor grabbed my hand. "C'mon, Miss Kelly. Let's go. First I want you to see my school exhibit. I made the poster."

We walked over to an elementary school exhibit, where Trevor's poster boldly proclaimed: BACK TO OUR ROOTS— SEE HOW OUR GARDENS GROW. The exhibit itself featured container gardens. Seedlings in foam egg cartons; larger plants in recycled cans, bottles, and jars.

"Trevor, that's a wonderful poster. I didn't know you were so talented."

We left the exhibit hall for the midway and found the necklace seller. Trevor counted out a dollar in change and soon was sporting a neon tube around his neck in blood moon orange.

"C'mon. Now we're going to ride the Ferris wheel."

"I don't know about that, Trevor."

"It's not real high. If you get scared, I'll be right next to you."

"Okay, Trevor. One time. But you have to promise me something."

"What's that?"

"No rocking the car when we get to the top. That makes me very nervous."

Trevor rolled his eyes. "Not even a little bit?"

"Zip, nada, none. Not even a wiggle."

"O-kay. I promise."

We joined the queue at the ticket booth. I bought a strip of ten tickets, tore off two for the Ferris wheel, and handed the rest to Trevor. "Have fun at the fair."

"Wow. Thanks, Miss Kelly."

The line at the Ferris wheel was the longest of all the rides. Finally it was our turn. Trevor climbed in first and slid over to the far side of the car. After I got in next to him, the attendant flipped down the safety bar and snapped it into place. I clutched the bar with both hands and hung on for dear life as the car began to move.

We edged upward only a few feet off the ground, just far enough to allow the car behind us to discharge its passengers and take on new riders.

And so it went, car by car, until we were almost to the top.

Trevor was squirming with excitement. "Look! You can see everything!" He pointed at the exhibit hall at the far end of the fairground.

I wanted to scream, "Trevor, sit still and keep your hands on the safety bar." But I bit my tongue and, one hand at a time, wiped my dripping palms on my shorts before grasping the safety bar once more.

While we hung motionless in the air, I took a moment to enjoy the view—which was as spectacular as Trevor had promised—and focused on little details on the ground such as the lights of a black car parked near the trees on the far side of the exhibit hall.

As Trevor was shouting, "There's my mom. Look, Mom! I'm up here!," the Ferris wheel began turning slowly. The riders laughed and squealed as the wheel moved faster and faster.

When we were almost back at the top on the second time around, a muffled boom emanated from the area of the homestead house.

The fairground went completely dark and the Ferris wheel shuddered to an abrupt stop.

Trevor and I were stuck in the car at the very top.

# Chapter
# 39

"TREVOR, ARE YOU all right?" I could barely make out his face in the faint orange glow of his lightstick necklace.

"I'm okay. Don't be scared." I felt his small hand reach for mine. "You'll see. It'll be all right. My mom will get us down."

Below us the fairground had erupted in groans, shrieks, screams, shouts, and running footsteps. A minute or two later, as if on cue, car and truck lights were turned on and switched to bright, providing scanty illumination. From our vantage point at the top of the Ferris wheel we could see that the power outage was confined to the fairground. Too many extension cords and too few outlets, I thought to myself.

"Trevor! Where are you?" We heard Camille yelling from the base of the Ferris wheel.

"I'm at the top, Mom."

"Are you okay? Who's with you?"

"I'm okay. Miss Kelly is with me. I think she's scared."

"Hang on, Trevor. Stay in the seat with Kelly. The

cherry picker is coming over here to get you down."

We heard a second boom. A hundred feet away from us the homestead outhouse burst into flames. There were more screams, more footsteps, and shouts of "Where are the fire extinguishers?" and "Someone call the fire department." I saw several people running away from the fire area toward the exhibit hall.

Trevor clutched my hand. His palm was suddenly as wet as my own. I slid my free arm around him and hung on to the back of the seat to steady us.

"I want to get out of here," Trevor wailed.

"Sh-h-h-h, sweetie," I said, squeezing his hand. "We'll be down soon. Hear that rumble like thunder? That's the cherry picker coming to get us. While we're sitting here waiting, why don't you sing me a little song?"

"What should I sing?"

"How about something from the play you're in."

"I don't have any songs. The prince doesn't sing."

"You know all the songs from the video," I said. "Pick one of those."

In a small faltering voice, Trevor began singing. Then he paused. "I forget the words to the next part, but it goes like this: Dah dah d-a-a-h dah d-e-e dah dah."

My ears perked up like Minx's when she hears a cat food lid popping.

"Trevor, hum that last part again. Real slow."

"Which part?"

"The one you just did."

"This one? Dah dah d-a-a-h dah d-e-e dah dah."

"That's the one. Do it again."

While he hummed to me, the lightbulb inside my head exploded like a Macy's Fourth of July fireworks display. The events of the past month fell into place at last.

"Trevor, you *are* a prince!" I held him close as I leaned over the safety bar to look for Camille.

"Miss Kelly, you're rocking the car. Please stop. You made me promise not to do that."

The cherry picker slowly ascended to our car. Our savior was the Ag Fair worker I had seen earlier in the evening hanging the banner. I helped Trevor climb into the basket first, then scrambled in after him.

When we were back on the ground, Camille pulled Trevor into her arms and held him tight.

"Camille, where's Benjamin?" I asked.

"I don't know, Kelly. I haven't seen him all evening."

"Tell him I'm looking for him." I took off in the direction of the exhibit hall.

The little bridge was clogged with people trying to get away from the fairground. I scrambled down the bank and worked my way gingerly along the rutted surface of the dry gut. The half-moon was more hindrance than help, doubling the size of shadows while offering little in the way of true illumination.

I scrambled out of the gut close to Central Factory. Then headed across the open field for the north end of the exhibit building. Feeling my way along the outside wall, I turned the northwestern corner of the building. There was the black car I'd spotted from the top of the Ferris wheel. The trunk was open and crammed with twenty-five-pound bags of fertilizer. I turned to go back the way I'd come, hoping to circle around to the front of the building.

The driver jumped out of the car, sprinted after me, tackled me, and threw me to the ground before I'd covered ten feet.

I struggled to get free. A hand was clamped over my mouth before I could scream for help. I opened my mouth wide and bit down. Hard. Hard enough to leave deep teethmarks and draw blood. The hand was instantly withdrawn. Then I felt a fist make contact with my face.

The next thing I heard were the sounds of a revving engine and a car burning rubber out of the fairground.

Then I saw a bobbing light approaching from the direction of Central Factory and heard Benjamin's voice. "Kelly, are you there? Where have you been? I've been looking for you all night."

# Chapter
## 40

BENJAMIN SHONE HIS flashlight on my face. "What happened to you?"

I wobbled when I tried to stand and reached for Benjamin's hand to steady myself. "There's no time to talk. Where's your car? Benjamin, there's a killer on the loose! I was dead wrong. It wasn't Miss Maude!"

He pulled me off the ground and we ran to his car, parked a few feet away. I told him where we were going and why. He nodded curtly, then drove hell-bent for leather out of the fairground, lights flashing and siren screaming in pursuit of the black car.

My face was swelling and I was having a hard time seeing what was happening on the road ahead of me. It looked as if we were following three red taillights. I shook my head to clear my vision, a move I instantly regretted.

Cars swerved and dove into the bush alongside the road as we tore through the St. Chris countryside toward Isabeya. Once we got to town, we slowed to a crawl in the single-lane Friday night traffic on Kongens Gade. Benjamin thumped the steering wheel impatiently and muttered under his breath.

Our chase ended at Government House.

Benjamin pulled his gun from its holster as we ran through the automatic driveway gate before it swung shut.

"Halt! You're under arrest!" said Benjamin, pointing his gun at the figure emerging from a black car.

"One move and I'll fire," said another voice.

Chris Edwards looked from side to side with an amused expression on his face. "Will someone please tell me what this is all about?"

Michael emerged from the shadows, his gun pointed at Chris's heart. "Hands up. Now." We all saw the blood and teethmarks on his right palm when Chris raised his hands.

Then we heard another voice, from a figure approaching from the courtyard. "What the devil has been going here? Chris, I think you've got some explaining to do."

Chris took one look at the governor, threw back his head, and bayed at the moon.

# Chapter
# 41

BACKUP POLICE UNITS arrived and Chris was taken into custody.

There was some squabbling between Benjamin and Michael as to which charges Chris would be facing first. Local murder or federal drug trafficking. It was like watching two kids play a game of scissors, paper, stone.

Evidence covering both charges was retrieved from the trunk of the black car and Chris's office. Buried in the down-island fertilizer bags was enough cocaine to blanket St. Chris in a layer of white. In the wine bottles was sufficient disulfiram to make anyone who drank it very, very sick. A prescription bottle of Antabuse bearing the governor's name was found in Chris's desk drawer.

"Kelly, we're also going to need your dental records," said Benjamin.

"My what? What for?"

"Assault charges." Benjamin began to laugh. "Chris demanded a tetanus shot before he was taken to jail."

We spent an hour talking with the governor in his private quarters. He listened quietly and drank nothing but Perrier with a twist of lime. When we were at last finished, he raised his hand to speak.

"When my wife died two years ago, I couldn't cope with the loss. I suppose it's no secret that I haven't been attending to business as I should. Dr. Williams prescribed Antabuse to curb my drinking, but it wasn't what I wanted and I threw the bottle away. I only wanted to forget. Chris took over completely and it was he who suggested after Hurricane Gilda that I go to a private alcohol rehab facility in the States. He said he would cover for me and no one would ever suspect I was gone. I left here the day after Christmas for a two-month stay. I wasn't due back here for another week."

"Excuse me, sir," I said, "what made you decide to come back tonight?"

"I read in the *New York Times* that we have visitors arriving tomorrow morning," the governor said with a small smile. "It was hell getting back here, the flights were booked solid. But I came in tonight on the last flight from San Juan and caught a taxi to town at the airport. The driver didn't even recognize me. Now, will someone please tell me what's on the agenda for this royal visit?"

We spent the next half hour detailing the events of the royal visit while the governor took notes.

"Chris had a real talent for delegating responsibility. And usurping authority," said the governor. "I should have known better than to keep him on, but I was in no shape to face the facts." He turned to Benjamin. "I've been putting off filling a vacancy in the police department. One of my last official acts as governor will be to appoint you as the chief of detectives. I should have done it months ago."

"You're not resigning?" said Benjamin.

"When the scandal about Chris hits the news, I won't

have any choice," replied the governor. "It's time I retired to private life. I've been a public servant for over forty years."

"The Monday edition of the *Telegraph* goes to press tomorrow and the stories have already been written," I said. We all smiled, well aware of the idiosyncrasies of the weekend edition of our local newspaper. "Benjamin, can't we keep a lid on this until next week? After the royal visit is over? I can promise you there won't be a leak at WBZE."

Michael motioned to Benjamin and they huddled in a corner of the room.

The governor looked at my swollen, bruised, dirt-streaked face. "Did Chris do that to you?"

"Yes."

"I am truly sorry." He rose from his chair and went into the bathroom, returning with a towel which he filled with ice and handed to me. "Perhaps this will help until you can get to the hospital. I will personally take care of your medical expenses."

"We've decided to transfer Chris to a federal facility in Puerto Rico first thing Saturday morning, before the Queen arrives," said Michael. He pointed to the governor's desk a few feet away. "May I use your phone?"

"Moving Chris will curtail any idle gossip here this weekend," said Benjamin. "He'll spend tonight in solitary confinement."

Michael hung up the phone and looked at his watch. "It's show time, Mama. I've got to get to the station."

I turned to the governor. "I know Chris was very clever, but how was he going to explain your absence at the events this weekend?"

"By announcing that I was indisposed and he was designated to take my place," replied the governor with a rueful smile. "Those were my standing instructions."

# Chapter
## 42

MICHAEL ZOOMED OFF to WBZE on his Harley. Benjamin and I went back to the fairground after promising Michael we would meet him later at the station.

"Come on, Kelly, we need to get back to the fairground," said Benjamin. "Camille and Trevor will be looking for me."

"I want to talk to Miss Maude first," I said. "Do you think it's too late?"

"That depends," said Benjamin. "Too late for what?"

"An apology."

"It's never too late to apologize to the ones we love," said Benjamin, "but this isn't the time."

"But I was so wrong about her. How could I have thought she was guilty of murder? I must have been out of my mind."

Benjamin took my hand in his. "It's easy to make a false assumption when you don't have all the facts. This will stay between us, Miss Maude will never know. That I promise you. We have no need to ever speak of it again."

Tears welled as I squeezed Benjamin's hand in gratitude.

When we arrived back at the fairground, power had been completely restored. Benjamin parked the police car and went to look for Camille and Trevor.

I walked over to the homestead house, where the building crew was surveying the fire damage. The outhouse was history. A charred ruin.

Maubi shook his head. "We never should have stored the paint cans in there. The sun on that tin roof was too hot. Just look at the back of the house."

It looked exactly as if a paint bomb had exploded—which in fact it had—hurling globs of paint onto the roof and back wall of the homestead house. Aside from the paint, the rest of the house was intact and undamaged.

"Who's got a phone?" I said. Three people reached for cell phones.

I called my ex-husband. "Pete, I know it's the middle of the night. And I'm sorry if the phone woke the baby, but I really need your help."

As I shut off the phone, Benjamin arrived with Camille and Trevor.

"There you are, Kelly," said Camille. "Did Ben ever find you? I told him you were looking for him. But that was hours ago."

Benjamin winked at me over Camille's head.

"Miss Kelly," said Trevor, "you lost your green necklace. I saw one on the ground near the end of the exhibit building, but it was all smashed. I'll buy you a new one tomorrow."

Now I knew how Chris had followed me so easily in the dark.

"Come on, Trevor, we have to go home and get you to bed," said Camille. "It's way past your bedtime and tomorrow is a big day."

I hugged Trevor and kissed him good night.

"What happened to your eye, Kelly?" asked Camille. "Did you run into something?"

"You could say that," I replied.

"Ben, try to get home at a decent hour, will you?" Camille took Trevor by the hand and they walked to the parking lot.

Within an hour, a truck from Island Lumber pulled into the fairground with Pete at the wheel.

The building crew worked for most of the night, tearing down the remains of the old outhouse, building a new one, and repairing the paint job on the roof and back wall of the homestead house.

Maubi emptied the kerosene lamps and refilled them with colored water. "We don't need any more fire. Things be hot enough around here already."

After the rest of the building crew had gone home to bed, Benjamin, Maubi, and I unpacked the boxes Amelia had brought and arranged the items in the lean-to kitchen. We hung the cooking utensils from nails on the wall and put the dishes on the open shelf. Wooden spoons went into an old coffee can, rusted with age. The coal pot for cooking was stored in a corner. Maubi hammered one last nail into the wall. On it he hung a battered blue enameled kettle.

"Alveena teach me how to make maubi in this very kettle," he said. "It's high time she got it back."

# Chapter
## 43

THE BELL IN the Anglican church was tolling four when Benjamin and I walked into WBZE.

I handed Michael a frosty Tuborg. "Compliments of Maubi. To celebrate the Queen's arrival." Benjamin and I opened our own bottles. I put the rest of the six-pack in the refrigerator.

"Ben, the chopper from San Juan will be here at six-thirty," said Michael. "We need to be at the airport by seven at the latest. Then the marshals will take over."

"Okay by me," replied Benjamin. "I will be very glad to see the back of Chris Edwards."

"Now," said Michael, "is someone going to fill me in?"

Benjamin and I looked at each other. "You start, Kelly," he said.

"I don't know about the drug business," I said, "but I think the rest of it began at Miss Maude's house the Saturday morning she invited us all to the royal dinner."

Benjamin nodded.

"Miss Lucinda was in her cups, and after Chris arrived

to discuss plans for the royal visit, she made a very pointed remark about the governor's drinking problem and hinted that if he had a wife maybe we'd see more of him. It went completely over my head at the time. But other people said pretty much the same thing. That the governor was seldom seen, or always in meetings with Chris. Who was I to doubt it?

"Then we come to Miss Maude's dinner party. Chris brought the wine, but it wasn't served until the end of the evening with the dessert. That night everyone was in and out of the kitchen. Miss Lucinda was the only one who didn't sample the champagne when Chris made the toast to Miss Maude. I heard her mutter, 'Champagne makes me windy,' and she put her glass down untasted. We all got sick, but thought it was fish poisoning."

"I'll bet Chris didn't drink the wine either," said Benjamin.

"Miss Maude was devastated about what happened at her dinner party and talked about canceling the royal dinner. Benjamin pulled her trash from the dump and discovered that the fish she served was dolphin, which Victoria told me is perfectly safe and not a carrier of ciguatera. But the fact remained that we were all sick, which we then concluded had to be the flu. Ciguatera, flu? Who could tell the difference?"

"Mama, I told you the odds of nine people getting sick at the same time were damned slim."

"But only eight were sick. Benjamin, you said that although Miss Lucinda claimed to be sicker than anyone, you thought it was only a case of juniper berry flu because she'd consumed most of a bottle of Tanqueray that night."

I paused for a swallow of beer. "Other people were getting sick, too. But since we all had the same symptoms, it made the flu story all the more plausible."

"Who else got sick, Mama?"

"First, Victoria. Then Jerry, Abby, Paul, and Margo. After they'd had dinner at Jerry's. Heidi didn't get sick that night, but she'd had the flu a couple of weeks earlier and wasn't drinking at all or eating very much. Michael, you remember when Heidi was sick? The night Jerry showed up at my house when we were having the fondue dinner with Paul and Margo."

"Right. I forgot about that."

"What we all had in common—aside from contact with Chris—was the taste of garlic and the fact that booze didn't sit very well in our systems after we'd recovered. Benjamin, you told me that was the reason you were drinking club soda the afternoon at Dockside when I went to see how Victoria was feeling. And Michael, you complained of a headache after one Carlsberg. I felt queasy myself after one beer. Margo had to leave the Lime Tree after a Bloody Mary at lunch."

"Now we come to Miss Lucinda's death. When her body was discovered, she'd choked to death on her own vomit and there was a faint smell of garlic in the air. I naturally assumed, that like everyone else, she had the flu. And that's what I told Dr. Williams. But he knew better."

"Take a break, Kelly, you're getting hoarse," said Benjamin. "How about getting us those extra beers?"

I gathered the warm empties and replaced them with full cold ones. "Then Dr. Williams had his fatal car accident the weekend following Miss Lucinda's funeral. When Benjamin and I looked at Dr. Williams's notes on Miss Lucinda's death, that's when I saw the word 'disulfiram' for the first time."

"What's that?" said Michael.

"Antabuse," said Benjamin. "He prescribed the drug for the governor."

"In the *Physicians' Desk Reference* I read that the taste of garlic is one of the side effects of Antabuse," I said.

"So Chris doped the wine the night of Miss Maude's dinner," said Michael.

"He tiefed the cork when he rinsed out the bottle and wiped it clean of prints" added Benjamin.

"Right. And I'll bet he also doped the wine that Victoria and he were sampling at Dockside for the royal lunch the night she got sick. And the bottle Jerry served to Abby, Margo, and Paul."

"Busy guy," said Michael. "Sounds to me like he was doing everything possible to make sure the royal visit didn't come off."

"I think so, too," said Benjamin. "But he made it look like he was doing everything to make it a success."

"Maubi once commented that Chris never rolled up his sleeves to make a sweat," I said.

"The royal visit was getting in the way of his drug deal. But the visit had gone beyond his control," said Michael. "Mama, you were the one who clued me as to where and when the deal was coming down. I owe you for that."

"What did I do?"

"My informants told me it was happening this weekend. Then you said the down-island vendors were setting up for the fair Friday night. Perfect time and place. Good camouflage, lots of people, lots of activity, everyone busy doing their own thing and not paying much attention to anyone else."

I turned to Benjamin. "Was the power outage for real?"

"We'll never know, but the outhouse fire wasn't." He reached in his pocket and handed me a piece of twisted metal that had once been a key. "I found this in the wreckage. There were only two keys. The one I gave to Chris to have gold-plated for the Queen and the one I kept." He jingled a key ring. "Here's mine."

"It's getting late, Mama. You need to go home and do something about that eye. You've got a real shiner going."

"Wait a minute," said Benjamin. "What about Miss Lucy's death? Kelly, how did you tie Chris into that?"

"Three people helped me solve that one eventually. Miss Lucinda, Elodia, and Trevor."

"Trevor?" said Benjamin. "What did he do?"

"He sang to me when we were stuck on top of the Ferris wheel. But he couldn't remember all the words."

"This I've got to hear," said Benjamin.

"We've all heard the rumor that when she was a young woman, Miss Lucinda had a dalliance with the Prince of Wales, later crowned King Edward the Eighth, after his abdication known as the Duke of Windsor."

"I never thought that was true," said Michael.

"Well, it was. I saw the proof with my very own eyes in Miss Lucinda's photo album," I said. "But it was Miss Lucinda herself who gave me the first clue. That Saturday morning at Miss Maude's when Chris was there, Miss Lucinda stared at Chris and mumbled, 'You look like my David.' Miss Lucinda was so nearsighted that to her Chris probably did resemble the prince. Or at least her memory of him. Then Elodia said that Miss Lucinda was in her sitting room the afternoon before she died, humming happily to herself and looking at her photo albums. Elodia tried to sing the song to me. But she didn't know what it was called and didn't know the words. The poor dear couldn't carry a tune in a bucket. Then Trevor sang the same song to me on top of the Ferris wheel."

"Kelly, will you cut to the chase?" said Benjamin.

"What's the song, Mama?" said Michael.

I grinned and said, " 'Someday My Prince Will Come.' "

"That damned *Snow White* video," said Benjamin. "I've heard that song so many times in the past few weeks I don't even hear it anymore." He reached into his pocket and pulled out a small velvet bag. "That explains why I found this hidden in the back of Chris's desk drawer."

He opened the pouch and pulled out a Cartier platinum and diamond wristwatch. I knew at a glance it was the real thing. Engraved on the back were the words: "To Lucy. Forever. David."

"I think that belongs to Miss Maude now," I said.

"I'll see that she gets it," said Benjamin. "It's too valuable to be left in an evidence locker. We've got Chris cold on drug possession and assault. It's only a matter of time until he confesses to the murders of Miss Lucy and Dr. Williams."

"Mama, it's almost six. Can you cover for me until the weekend guy gets here?"

Michael and Benjamin left the studio for the airport. I looked at my paint-spattered hands and chipped nail polish and hoped I had enough time for a quick repair job before I had to get back to town for the Queen's arrival.

As I drove down Kongens Gade on the way home to change clothes and slather makeup on my eye, I saw Victoria crossing the street from Dockside toward Government House.

I honked and slowed down. "Good morning, Vic. I see you're getting an early start. Did you ever get that Government House pass you needed?"

Victoria smiled. "The governor called me himself first thing this morning. He apologized for the confusion and said that Chris was indisposed and that he'd be taking over Chris's duties for the royal visit. I'm going over to set the tables for the royal lunch now. I'll see you at the wharf in a couple of hours."

# Chapter
## 44

UNDER A CLOUDLESS sky the color of the finest lapis, St. Chris residents, tourists, and the media crowded the wharf and shoreline of Isabeya in anticipation of the arrival of Queen Margrethe and her husband, Prince Henrik.

Miss Maude and the governor of St. Chris stood arm in arm next to the flagpole where the red and white Danish flag once again fluttered in the morning breeze. It was the same spot where Miss Maude had stood, wearing a new pink dress and clutching her mother's hand, in 1917 when the Dannebrog was lowered and St. Chris ceased to be a Danish colony.

The crowd gasped in awe and wonder when the three-masted *Danmark* came into view under full sail with Danish sailors in fresh white uniforms standing at attention in the rigging, accompanying the royal yacht *Dannebrog* bearing the royal visitors.

Miss Maude smoothed the skirt of her new pink flowered silk dress and adjusted her pink straw cartwheel hat. With a joyous welcoming smile lighting her face, she walked to the end of the wharf to greet her Queen.